gettin' hooked

Nyomi Scott
gettin' hooked

KIMANI
TRU™

GETTIN' HOOKED

ISBN-13: 978-0-373-83086-2
ISBN-10:   0-373-83086-6

www.KimaniTRU.com

Printed in U.S.A.

KIMANI
tru
™

FRESH. CURRENT. AND TRUE TO YOU

Dear Reader,

What you're holding is very special. Something fresh, new and true to your unique experience as a young African-American! We are proud to introduce a new fiction imprint—Kimani TRU. You'll find Kimani TRU speaks to the triumphs, problems and concerns of today's black teens with candor, wit and realism. The stories are told from your perspective and in your own voice, and will spotlight young, emerging literary talent.

Kimani TRU will feature stories that are down-to-earth, yet empowering. Feel like an outsider? Afraid you'll never fit in, find your true love or have a boyfriend who accepts you for who you really are? Maybe you feel that your life is a disaster and your future is going nowhere? In Kimani TRU novels, discover the emotional issues that young blacks face every day. In one story, a young man struggles to get out of a neighborhood that holds little promise by attending a historically black college. In another, a young woman's life drastically changes when she goes to live with the father she has never known and his middle-class family in the suburbs.

With Kimani TRU, we are committed to providing a strong and unique voice that will appeal to *all* young readers! Our goal is to touch your heart, mind and soul, and give you a literary voice that reflects your creativity and your world.

Spread the word…Kimani TRU. True to you!

Linda Gill
General Manager
Kimani Press

KIMANI PRESS™

To all the girls who are trying to find their way through the craziness and hardships of daily life, trying to make smart decisions when the world is so complicated, and trying to chase dreams even when it feels nearly impossible.
The whole world is yours. Believe in yourself and you can be anything and everything you ever wanted.
More!

Have inner strength and always be true to yourself.

Nyomi

Acknowledgment

Thank you to my Sadie, who read chapter after chapter as I wrote, always asking for more. You laughed, cried, and became friends with the characters. I thank you for your encouragement and comments. I love you, my sweets. Always, "Sadie Baby" to me.

Thank you to my Rinkie-Dinkie Princess Girl, Tonysha. Thank you for catching my errors and double checkin' my slang. I would hate to have something be whack when it was meant to be off the chain. I adore you.

CHAPTER 1

FIND YOUR SOUL MATE

I hate those whack little pop-up ads. The ones that show up right when you're in the middle of something else, and when you try to close it you end up at their freakin' site. As I stared at the hand-holding couple advertising their find-your-perfect-soul-mate service, I became even more irritated.

Find Your Soul Mate. "Riiiight…what I need is a prom date," I said to the pair grinning back at me in the pop-up ad as I was trying to do my MySpace.com updates. Maybe that's the reason I resented this ad more than others. Not only had my 'net security failed to do its thing, but the pop-up advertised what I didn't have, and that was a date.

Biting my bottom lip, I clicked the red X again, this time making the image disappear. I was straight trippin' if I thought the couple was actually in love. More like they were models, paid to make me feel like I was lacking just what they could offer.

Not that I needed a freakin' soul mate, but a date would've been nice. And as senior prom approached, one fact wasn't fading no matter how I tried to ignore it: I didn't have one.

I took a deep breath and swallowed the lump in my throat. I knew the reason I was still dateless. It's hard to get excited about dudes I've known since elementary. Sure, there are some fine guys at my school, but the crushes I've had on them came and went before we ever got to high school. Besides, the decent-looking ones either have dated or messed with most of my friends. That puts them off-limits. Can't be with my friends' exes.

I tapped my fingers in time with Chris Brown's hip-hop rhythm as I read over the MySpace profile changes I'd made, then hit Save. Checking my mail, I saw I had four new messages that had come in while I was making my updates. Two different invites to hit the movies Friday night. A message from one of my girls telling me that she'd put a prom dress on hold at the mall even if she didn't have a date yet. And a quick hi from my cousin, Kayla.

Scrolling across the top eight on my Friends list, I took the link over to Kayla's page, then moved the cursor down to where she had some pictures posted of her friends from school. Though we lived only a mile apart, she was in another district so we ended up going to different high schools. We hung out a lot, but we had different friends.

She had one friend that did it for me. Maurice Simms— a boy I've had a thing for ever since he moved here.

I wouldn't mind gettin' hooked up with him. Truth was, if I had the nerve, I'd have told Kayla about it way back and hoped she could arrange it. Instead I kept my feelings for him to myself.

I sighed, settling the cursor over his image. The boy was *hot*. Crowded into a picture in front of Kayla's house, Maurice was taller than the other guys, his shoulders broader. His smile revealed these little dimples in his face. Seeing the image, I felt like his dark eyes were looking right at me.

FIND YOUR SOUL MATE

Was this some kind of joke? I mean, Norton, are you asleep on the job? I wasn't supposed to be getting pop-ups at all, but the same one in less than five minutes? Was it trying to rub salt in my prom-dateless wound? Grinding my teeth, I closed the window and then signed out of MySpace.

Though I could spend a couple hours looking at Maurice's fine face, I planned on heading to Kayla's house to hang with her today. Besides, going over there meant I might get to see Maurice in person since he lived across the street.

I rifled through my pack right quick to make sure I had everything I needed, then flung it over my shoulder and headed out of my room, stopping at my grandma's door. Since my dad was an airline pilot—gone three times more than he was home—he'd moved my grandma in with us after my grandpa passed. He'd said it was so I wouldn't be alone so much, but I knew it was so Gram wouldn't. I was cool with it. Before grandpa died, I mostly lived at their place anyway when my dad was gone on flights.

I cleared my throat, something making it feel clogged.

"Gram, I'm goin' to Kayla's now, all right?" I leaned into her room and squinted. The only light came off the TV; the windows were covered in shades and thick curtains.

"Where, Imani?" She hit the mute button and turned her recliner toward the door.

I took a deep breath. "Kayla's."

She pursed her lips into a sour face, but turned back toward the TV without saying anything. I knew she didn't like my cousin's family. Kayla's mom was my momma's sister, and my momma decided to bail right before my first birthday. I guess having a kid wasn't what she'd expected.

No one on my dad's side of the family acknowledged them, but they never kept me from having a relationship with them, either. It's not like my momma kept in touch with her family and not me. She pretty much deserted all of us, and really, I don't give a shit. To me she doesn't exist. But even after almost seventeen years, my grandma couldn't forget.

"Do you want me to get you somethin' to eat first, Gram?" Her eyes were real sensitive to light, so she didn't venture out of her room much. Sometimes she wouldn't even eat unless I brought it to her.

"Your daddy called," she said, changing the subject.

"Yeah? Is he comin' in soon?"

"Didn't say when. Just checking on you."

"I'm all right," I mumbled, unable to keep the sorrow from my tone. If I could hear it, I'm sure Gram could, too. Not wanting to talk about it, I walked away from her door and headed toward the kitchen to make her something to eat even though she hadn't answered me.

I dropped my bag on a stool in front of the counter. The black granite countertop reflected the gloss of tears shimmering in my eyes. As I made her a sandwich, I tried to shake off the dull ache of missing my dad, of wishing he were around more. It was only at quiet, lonely times like this that I allowed myself to wonder if my momma split because of something he did, or because she couldn't deal with me being half-black.

Before he died, Grandpa always pointed out that she'd left just when my hair started to curl up. I touched one dark ringlet, wrapped it around my fingers, then closed my eyes for a sec, inhaling my conditioner. It's not like I could control the texture. And I wouldn't change it anyhow. Not for her. Not for anyone. I'm proud of who I am, brown skin, round ass, curly hair and all.

Tucking the curl behind my ear, I focused on making Gram's food. I had enough to think about being manless with prom approaching—I didn't need to be rehashing why my momma straight-up left me. Swallowing any lingering sadness, I knew what I needed to fix the dateless problem. Maurice. My heart sped up a little, thinking of him always did funny freakin' things to me.

I poured Gram a glass of iced tea, put her sandwich on a plate and suppressed the tears. Plastering a grin on my face, I took her the sandwich. "Gram, I made you somethin' to eat."

"Thanks, baby."

"I'm goin' now."

"Stay at her house. You're a pretty girl, Imani. Boys are going to want things from you."

I didn't need to ask what kind of things she was talking about. This was the standard warning I got when I was about to go out. No matter where I was headed.

Watch out for them boys.

Oh, I was checking them out all right. In a quick minute, I'd be checking out Maurice. "I'll be careful, Gram," I said, kissing her cheek. Some things were best left unsaid.

Back in the kitchen, I retrieved my backpack and stuck a water bottle in the side pocket, plopped the tiny iPod buds into my ears, slid on my stunna shades—they made me look gooood—and headed out the door.

It was on the fifteen-minute walk that my mind started swirling out of control. With my music on shuffle, the love songs by various artists pulsed in my ears, each one reminding me what I was missing.

If I wanted to be hooked up with Maurice before prom, then I was going to have to do something about it. Do nothing; get nothing. 'Bout time I got my scruff up and did something that'd make Maurice my man.

While Mariah Carey belted out a tune, all I could think about was Maurice dressed in a tux, a tiny pink rose pinned to his lapel. His smile really focused on me. Maurice there for me. With me.

Maurice as my prom date.

A lump formed in my throat, making it hard to swallow. My chest felt tight as my breathing became fast. Prom night was supposed to be the night. So many of my girls had talked about giving it up—the ones who hadn't already—on prom night. And though I wouldn't do it with just anyone, with the right mood—the right guy—I just might. It was the prom, the night that sends us off to the rest of our lives.

I sighed, sloshing my K-Swiss sneakers along the rain-dampened sidewalk, kicking at pebbles as they littered my path. The sky was gray, laden with moisture, and it clung to my skin and hair like dew on the morning grass. Though the air was cold, I felt warm in just my hip-hugging jeans and oversize sweatshirt. And the heat only seemed to rise the closer I got to Kayla's.

And to Maurice's.

I swear, I go to my cousin's house at least three times a week. And though I always slowed down as I passed Maurice's in hopes of getting a glimpse of him, I never felt anxious and excited before.

But today, that's just how I was feeling. That and being bugged by a little nugget of an idea that was trying to take shape in my mind.

Find Your Soul Mate...the pop-up image kept invading my thoughts. And the actors, the happy couple in the ad. The way they held hands and looked into each other's eyes. That's the kind of affection I wanted.

A guy *that* into me.

At seventeen, a senior in high school, I wasn't really looking for the soul mate thing, but replace that with *Find Your Dream Date,* and I'd so be there. I wasn't alone. Not only had my girls complained about their lack of prom date choices, but Kayla had commented on the same freakin' thing. When you live in the suburbs like we do, all the same kids end up at the same schools. Unless someone new moves in, it's the same old, same old.

I have had the same friends since kindergarten. That's all good, but when it comes to hot guys, well, you're limited. What we needed was something like MySpace where we could see each other's profiles, but everyone on it would be local. Can't exactly take a dude from across the country to prom night—a night that is supposed to be special.

Combine a locals-only MySpace thing with Find Your Dream Date and I'd have the perfect prom date hook-up service.

I stopped walking.

The idea taking a solid shape. We needed a Web site. A Web site where we could meet people from other local high schools and find the right date we couldn't get on our own—or at our own schools.

Prom was a little more than two months away—I had just enough time to get the idea off the ground, but I'd need help. Kayla's. Her dad, my uncle Rob, owned a software company, giving Kayla access to all sorts of computer stuff.

I pulled the buds from my ears and tucked the iPod

into my backpack, then slipped my bag over both shoulders. And took off at a jog. It was just a few blocks farther, but I was doped up on this idea and wanted to share right quick.

When I reached their court, I slowed down a little, and sneaked a glance toward Maurice's place. His garage door was open and an abandoned lawn mower was in his driveway. Just as I reached Kayla's walk, I caught a glimpse of Maurice from the corner of my eye. Wearing sweats and a white tee, he was getting a little hyphie coming out of his garage, dancing toward the mower.

Doing his own thing, he didn't notice me standing mesmerized across the street. Good thing, too, since I didn't doubt I was looking pretty freakin' stupid there with my mouth gaped open and drooling over his hot bod.

The sound of the mower starting up snapped me out of my messed-up daze. Taking a deep breath, I followed the stone path around the side of the house and let myself in through the sliding glass door.

"Hey, cuz," Brandon said, looking up from the comic books he had scattered across the glass table.

"Hi, Bran. Kayla here?"

"Room." He indicated with a nod of his head, then turned his attention back to the open pages.

At ten, my cousin Brandon cared only about three things—comic books, PlayStation 2 and football.

Though he had no interest in girls, he was a cutie and I bet it wouldn't be long before he had hordes of little bebopper chicks ringing his phone.

I didn't say anything to Brandon as I left the kitchen and headed up the stairs. Turning down the hall, I walked toward Kayla's room.

The door was half open, and I could hear her talking to someone. Tapping my knuckles against the wood, I opened it farther and stuck my head inside, scanning her tie-dye digs to see who she was chatting with.

Catching my eye, she grinned and pointed to the phone tucked between her cheek and ear. I entered her bedroom, moved to the giant beanbag chair and plopped down, dropping my pack to the floor by my feet.

My heart was racing with agitation the longer she stayed on the phone. I could tell by her end of the conversation she was talking to one of her girls who was having the same problem as me with her approaching senior ball: no date.

Tapping my toes and trying to be patient, I resisted the urge to tell her to hurry up as I left the beanbag and went to the window. Kayla's voice turned into a fuzz of words, my focus now on Maurice, who did this little dance thing with his feet as he pushed the mower across his yard.

His muscles bunched beneath his T-shirt and from my distance, I could see the beads of sweat. A sheen formed on his forehead even in the cold of the winter day, surrounded by rain clouds. He looked freakin' sexy.

Balling my hands into fists, I decided I'd eyed him long enough. Time to make the boy mine.

"What up, Imani?"

Being startled brought me back from my Maurice-as-my-man fantasy. Reluctantly turning away from the window, I grinned, anxious to see the look on her face when I told her my plan.

"Do you have a prom date?"

She sighed, gritting her teeth as she rolled her eyes. "You know I don't, girl. Not yet."

"How 'bout gettin' hooked?"

CHAPTER 2

Kayla dropped the phone she'd been fiddling with to the bed beside her, and was staring at me all crazy-like. Her big blue eyes held a hint of confusion, but something else, too. Excitement maybe? "Get hooked with who, Imani?"

"Anyone you want."

"Usher?"

I grinned at her, knowing she was teasing and knowing no matter what I'd said Usher was out of the question. Unless she was dreaming.

"Sure, girl. Usher." I rolled my eyes upward, taking in the hunk posters covering her walls before my gaze landed on the light pink ceiling. Sucking air between my teeth caused her to burst into giggles.

"Who then?" The words were spoken between bursts of laughter.

"I don't know. Anyone you like."

She pursed her lips. "You. Are. Trippin'. Girl." Each word was said all slow and punchy, just to put a little extra emphasis on them. "You know I'm not interested in anyone at Creekside."

"Why?"

"You know why. I've known most of them dudes my whole life."

"Exactly."

"You losing brain cells or something? What exactly does *exactly* mean?"

"It means the boyfriend-material guys you know are played out. So what about somewhere else, then?"

She yanked the rubber band from her hair, smoothed out the long blond strands, then twisted them back into the band. "You're serious?" Her brows plunged together as she looked at me. I gave a slight nod and she went on. "You know I think some of your friends are hot, but I don't really know them."

"Would you want to?"

We stared at each other for a few seconds longer, my reflection in her pale eyes reminding me again just how different we were. Yet similar, too. I knew she'd be down before the words even popped out of her mouth.

"Sure. What about you? You dig anyone at Creekside? Have a thing for a guy you've never told me about?"

Shrugging, I glanced back out the window to where

Maurice was mowing the grass. The fact that Kayla didn't know that I was into Maurice was kind of weird, considering there wasn't much my cousin didn't know about me.

His white T-shirt was damp now, from sweat or the moisture hanging in the overcast sky, I was too far away to tell, but it made his dark skin visible through the material. His body was sculpted—toned like an athlete's. More perfect than the pictures hanging on my cousin's walls.

My heart was thumping, pounding my pulse all loud in my ears. I knew Kayla was saying something. Could hear her voice, but the words were drowned out by my reaction to Maurice's movements as he pushed the mower.

I stared at him even though I knew Kayla was waiting for a response—a response I was hesitant to give. The bed squeaked and I could sense her coming to my side.

Taking a deep breath, I tore my gaze away from Maurice before she realized who I was so freaking hung up on. Swallowing to clear the dryness in my throat, I turned back to her and moved away from the window, though the hunk-a-licious image of him wasn't easy to put from my mind.

"So?"

"Dunno." My smile widened as I evaded the question. Maurice was my secret, and there was something safe about keeping him there. Not telling may have kept me safe, but it also kept me single. I struggled to keep my voice normal and my breathing slow. To disguise a rising, irrational sense of panic.

"There's some fine-ass guys at Creekside, and lawdy knows I'm not getting a date from Howard. I'd get hooked up, too, with the right guy." Vague enough?

"So who's the right guy?"

Again I ignored her question, figuring my plan would straight-up distract her enough to keep her from badgering for an answer.

I sat down at her computer desk, flicking the mouse to bring it out of sleep mode. "Check this out." A few clicks later I had my updated MySpace profile up on the screen.

"Ooh, I like your changes." Her head bobbed to "Yo," the song I'd uploaded just an hour before. Kayla reached around me to scoop up a bottle of nail polish, then tapped it against her palm.

"Thanks. Just did 'em."

With a few more clicks the screen changed to the list of my likes and dislikes, info only people on my friends list would have access to. "But this is what I want you to see."

"Yeah?" She squinted, then slanted her face toward me. She was for sure skeptical, that was clear. "I've seen it all before, Imani, so what's it got to do with getting hooked up with someone?"

"What if we could see this info about guys from each other's schools? And what if they could see ours?"

"They can."

"But only people on friends lists. And, that could be anyone, from across the country. That's whack and does us no good finding prom dates. What if there was a way to keep this local? Just our two high schools."

"Like our own locals-only MySpace?"

"Yeah." Logging out of MySpace, I went to GoDaddy and typed in GettinHooked. The name was available.

"You wanna run a Web site?"

"No, not really. But I *do* wanna go to the prom with the right guy. Running our own hook-up system will let us check out boys first, and will let your friends meet mine. I know I have hella girls that are tired of the dudes at our school. And are still prom-dateless. You do, too."

"True."

"If we set up GettinHooked.com, we can have pictures and profiles. Our friends will be able to see what they like—and don't like—about each other, then can send us a message and asked to be hooked up."

"We'd set up the dates?"

"Yep." Glancing over my shoulder, I winked at her. She was still shaking the nail-polish bottle—the *tap-tap-tap* on beat with "Yo," which was still playing low in the background. "And we could even sit in on some of the first meetings, ya know, so no one gets freaked."

Kayla plopped back onto her bed, her blond hair flung out around her, and laughed. "I love it, Imani. I've got tons of friends that'll be game."

"Me, too. So?"

"So?"

"Should I buy the domain?"

"Hell, yeah, girl. Buy it."

"We'll still need a server."

"We can use my dad's and a basic template. It should be pretty easy to set up."

"Fa sheezy."

Reaching for my backpack, I retrieved the prepaid Visa my dad gave me. Since I was on my own a lot, he figured I needed to be able to take care of my own needs. Mostly, I think, he just didn't know how to deal with the girlie issues—things a momma shoulda handled. It was cool with me. Aside from food, I'd been shopping for clothes, makeup and *girlie* things on my own for years.

So long as I'm responsible about spending my scratch, he kept a nice-size balance available for me. Ten bucks wouldn't be a problem.

Closing my eyes, I took a steadying breath and ended up inhaling the sharp scent of nail-polish. I glanced at Kayla, who now sat on the floor with her back to the bed and her knees bent.

She painted her toenails.

I moved through the pages of GoDaddy, finding my way to the purchase page.

There was this crazy sizzle of energy creeping through my body as I typed in the info to secure the domain. A wound-up sensation of accomplishment and excitement that had my heart beating fast and my hands trembling—enough so that I had to think about the letters my fingers were striking and wipe my hands on my jeans a couple of times.

There was this feeling—this stupid feeling—twisting and turning in my gut, like something big was going to come of this. Like this idea was going to *blow up*.

And maybe—just maybe—this was the step needed to wind up with the guy I wanted.

Whatever it was, it felt good. Damned good. My lip, which I'd been worrying between my teeth, popped free, a smile taking over as the confirmation page slid into place on the monitor.

GettinHooked.com belonged to me.

Grinning, I forced myself to keep from looking out the window again, to keep my secret, secret. With my back to my cousin, I lowered my lids and focused on the sound of the mower humming in the background. That was my man out there. He just didn't know it yet. After a few minutes the sound of the engine sputtered, then stopped, but I kept my eyes closed hoping to hear what he'd be doing next.

"We all set?"

Startled, I gasped and turned toward Kayla.

"What's up with you today?"

"Not a thing," I lied, putting my Visa card back in pack. Something was definitely freaking me today, I just wasn't sure exactly why I was tripping. "All gravy, girl. GettinHooked.com is ours."

"That's hella tight."

"What now, computer geek?"

Kayla clicked her tongue, along with giving me an an eye roll. "Whatever." She got to her feet, careful to keep her toes up, and walked toward her door on her heels. "Now what? Now we go to my dad's office and get server space."

She hobbled back to her bed, grabbed the phone, then tossed it to me. "I'll set up the site. You start making calls."

We went downstairs and into her dad's office, spending the remainder of the afternoon there, playing with Web site templates and making phone calls.

The design we chose was simple; a pure black background so that once we had pictures of our friends to upload they'd really stand out.

Our home page announced what we were all about— *Prom date hook-ups.* We included a log-in feature where a name and high school ID number had to be entered in order to start checking out the profiles. We mimicked some of the features from MySpace we thought were important, but we also added some of our own.

We added a music plug-in and uploaded a shuffling of slow songs from my iPod. Once someone logged in they'd be taken to a page that divided the guys from the girls. Not that we had any yet, but the pictures would load four per page, and once clicked on, the link would take you to their complete profile page, giving all the details that'd help someone decide if they wanted the hook-up.

By the time we were done it was nearly dark, my ass was tired of sitting and my voice was tired of talking. A few hours in and we had hella friends hyped on the idea and ready to sign up as soon as our site went live.

Gathering my backpack, I retraced my steps through the kitchen. My auntie was there making dinner and invited me to stay, but I was ready to go.

Maybe because I'd been thinking about my momma leaving me, or the fact that I was really missing my dad, but I wasn't in the mood to hang with them and longed for the solitude and quiet of my own thoughts. My own space.

I was offered a ride home, but declined, kinda looking forward to the walk.

Outside the evening air had cooled, but rain held off. Streetlights had clicked on even though the sun hadn't quite set behind the clouds.

Maurice's garage was closed, causing a little pang of regret over not seeing him again. But I would. Soon.

As soon as GettinHooked.com was up and running, I planned on using it to my advantage. I grinned. What Kayla didn't know wouldn't hurt her, but the entire idea was loaded with ulterior motives. Mine. To make Maurice not just my prom date, but my man.

CHAPTER 3

"Can you see what they're doing?" Kayla asked, batting my hair out of the way and pressing her weight into my back.

Lawdy, Kayla and I must have looked like a couple of straight-up fools, kneeling behind a bush with discarded McD's bags tucked beneath our knees to keep them out of the mud. The ground was wet and getting wetter, the continued light rain causing all sorts of messed-up damage to my hair.

Sliding a hand over my head, I tried to tame the increasing frizz by tucking it into the baseball cap I'd snagged from my dad's room, but the wild curls had a mind of their own. "Shoulda braided it," I mumbled, glancing right quick at Kayla.

Her focus wasn't on me, but fixed across the parking lot to the strip of stores located in The Plaza, an outdoor mini-mall.

"Look," she whispered, jabbing me in the side with her elbow, "I think they're holding hands."

"Already? Is Missy a bopper?"

She shook her head. "She's not fast like that."

"If you say so," I replied, rolling my eyes and sucking air between my teeth.

Holding a branch down, I angled my body to see past the leaves and through the front window of Starbucks, where GettinHooked.com's first date hook-up was taking place.

Well, sort of. Missy was one of Kayla's girls. We had plenty of girls, all our friends had been hip. But getting dudes to sign up hadn't been as easy, so this date was kind of an experiment just to see how things would work.

And from the looks of things—fast or not—it was going just fine. Both had their hands on the table, but from our vantage point of spying from the shrubs, there was really no telling if they were really holding hands.

It didn't matter. Missy and Jason were there because Kayla and I had hooked them up. It gets better, too: they'd picked each other off our site profiles.

There was pride in that.

I could feel it in my chest, this warmth caused by the hype of accomplishment. "They're talking. And laughing."

"This is so tight." Kayla giggled. "I wonder who we'll hook up next."

With a shrug, I pushed to my feet and kicked my legs to work out the freakin' kinks in my knees. Clouds hugged the rooftops. The air was thick, scented with wet asphalt. The rain was picking up now; hella fat droplets splattered against the brim of my hat.

The water was starting to soak through my sweat-shirt, too, making me wish I'd followed Gram's advice and worn a weatherproof jacket. I suppressed a shiver as I adjusted my pack over both shoulders, then wrapped my arms around my middle.

"We need more people to sign up." Because Maurice hadn't yet, and he was *it* for me.

"It's going to take off."

I nodded. I knew she was right—just a feeling deep in my gut that'd been with me since I'd thought up this whole idea. "That's what I need to do. *Take off.* I'm freezing." We started walking toward the overhang of the strip mall buildings where we'd be protected from the rainfall.

"You coming back to my place?"

There was a long, hot shower calling out to me. And fresh clothes. "Nah. Heading home. I'll check you later, though."

"'Kay."

"Bye, girl."

We hugged right quick, then moved away from each other, our homes were in opposite directions, but the walk wasn't far for either of us.

I hadn't made it to the end of the mall when I spotted him.

Maurice stood with a few other fellas just outside The Body Shop, a workout center where he must have just finished up. His stance casual, he stood there all sexy like, half dressed, steam rising from his skin.

Crap, why now? I wondered, knowing I must look like a bum, with mud splattered on my knees, my sweatshirt soaked and my hair freakin' jacked up, half sticking out from under the ball cap.

Swallowing down the tightness in my throat, I tucked my chin to my chest and ignored the pounding *tha-thump* of my heartbeat. With a little luck, I'd be able to walk right on by and he wouldn't recognize me. With a big gulp of air burning in my lungs, I just kept putting one foot in front of the other, though it wasn't easy keeping my eyes off him. I wanted to stare, take in every inch of his bare chest and fine-ass body.

Come on, he was half naked, wearing nothing but baggy shorts—in the rain—with a duffel bag slung over one muscular shoulder. Freakin' normal to wanna look my fill.

He didn't say anything to me as I approached, just

kept talking to his friends, his voice deep and soothing. It drew my attention and I glanced up in his direction.

And he was looking right back at me, our gazes catching and holding for a sec. I felt the blush on my cheeks, the heat spreading down my neck, and I hoped like hell it wasn't near as bright as I feared.

He grinned, then gave this little *what's up* lift of his chin. It wasn't easy, but I forced a small smile as I kept walking. All those times I'd hoped he'd notice me, just look up and wave or do something. All those times he hadn't, until the one whack moment I was looking my worst.

Slanting my head, I looked away and kept going.

"Imani."

Riiight, now the sound of the rain was playing tricks on me. No way did Maurice just call to me. "You're trippin, girl," I murmured under my breath, forcing myself to not end up a fool by glancing back.

"Hey, Imani, lemme holla at you."

The fact that I didn't fall smack down on my face should be noted, because as I paused and turned slowly toward him, my knees were shaking hella bad. He jogged the short distance between us, until he was standing all close to me, just inches apart.

The warmth of his skin rolled across the space, along with the musky scent of sweat and the spice of cologne. My skin prickled. Closing my eyes, I gulped down the lump forming in my throat, then glanced up at him.

"H-hey, Maurice." Adjusting my backpack, I put one hand on each strap and held on tight, just so he wouldn't see my hands trembling.

"I wanted to ask you 'bout somethin'."

"Hmm?"

"Heard you were looking for a guy."

Looking for a guy? *Pullease...I'd found him.* I was looking right at him, into eyes so dark it was hard to tell the difference between his pupils and irises. Eyes that glistened with interest, and brightened with a smile that dug dimples into his cheeks.

He cleared his throat and eyebrows arched over those eyes I just couldn't seem to tear my gaze from. He licked his lips as his smile widened.

Staring into his eyes was one thing, at his lips was something else—suggested I wanted something. Which I did, but no way was I ready for him to know it. Trippin' wasn't nearly a strong enough word for how I was behaving.

"A g-g-guy?" I shook my head, not really sure what he was talking about.

"Or guys, I guess." Maurice adjusted the strap on his shoulder, bunching up his muscles as he moved.

"Guys?"

His brows pulled together, his narrowing for a sec. "I was talking to Kayla. She mentioned—"

"Oh, yeah. For our site." There was really something

wrong with me if just being next to him caused me to go all stupid and forget all my plans. "We need more dudes. You going to sign up?"

"Feeling it out." His voice dropped, low and husky, and there was something in the tone that caused a shiver to run down my spine. The sensation moved through my body with a visible tremble.

"You cold?" he asked, pulling the hood of my sweatshirt out from under my pack and adjusting it around my neck. "Wanna a lift home?"

With a nod, I responded, "Sure, beats walking in the rain."

Maurice nodded, then turned back toward the guys he'd left standing in front of The Body Shop, flashing them a peace sign. "I'm out, fellas."

They mumbled goodbyes back, but I wasn't really paying attention, my mind whirling around the fact that he'd left his boys to take me home.

"Ready?"

"Mmm-hmm."

Slanting his head toward the parking lot, he said, "This way." Then his hand settled on my back, just gentle like, and hardly noticeable since I was wearing my pack. But I knew it was there, the light contact making my stomach do all sorts of whacked-out flips.

Not more than five cars down the row, he paused by

a black Nissan Altima, his hand falling away as he dug in his duffel bag for the keys.

The disappointment was sharp and immediate, the need to step closer was straight-up crazy. Blinking hard, I took a breath and stepped in the other direction, toward the passenger side of the car.

The keys jingled, then the alarm beeped as he unlocked the doors.

"This is a hella nice ride."

"Thanks. An early graduation gift."

"Really early." Two months remained before Senior Prom; it'd be another couple of weeks after that until graduation.

Maurice just shifted his shoulders, but didn't look up. "True." He was riffling through his bag, then came up with a sweatshirt that he shrugged into.

A few minutes later we were sitting in his car, the heater blasting and the stereo pumped so loud that the bass pulsed through the seat and my body.

He asked, "Which way?" leaning toward me.

To be heard over the music, I guess, but he was so freakin' close I could feel the warmth of his breath on my ear and swooshing down my neck. There was a lump in my throat that had to be worked free before I could reply.

After giving him directions, we drove to the rhythm of the beats bumping from the speakers, but as we moved through the gates of my condo complex less than five minutes later, he leaned forward and lowered the tunes.

"Why don't you have a profile?"

"On GettinHooked.com?" *He'd checked?*

"Yeah."

"Just haven't really had time."

"What number?"

"218." I pointed the condo out.

"But you are?"

I didn't really want a profile. I didn't want other dudes checking me out—*aaalll riiight,* the checking out was cool, but I didn't wanna have to deal with guys wanting to get hooked up. There was one reason—one guy—I wanted.

And he was sitting next to me.

Biting my lip, I thought over all the freakin' reasons I'd given Kayla for the skipping out on MySpace and starting GettinHooked. Fishing for a good one, I only came up with "Yeah, I'm into gettin' hooked, too." Lame.

"Don't know why ya need it, girl. You look hella good. You're crackin'." He'd pulled into a parking spot and put his car in Park, but hadn't turned off the engine.

I was straight-up thankful for the fact that it didn't look like he was getting out. But I needed to. I needed fresh air. Cool, fresh air to chill out the heat flaming on my skin. "Thanks," I said, knowing my voice cracked.

Glancing from my condo back toward Maurice, I realized junk was about to flow from my lips I wasn't ready for yet. Like telling him just how hot I thought he was. Like confessing the reason I'd delayed setting up my whack little profile was because I'd been waiting for him to do his so I could match it up to mine.

"I should jet." I opened the door and had one foot out when his hand settled over mine, warm and firm.

"Imani."

Gulping in a deep breath, then letting it out slowly, I turned to look at him. "Yeah?"

"I'll do your site thang."

I just stared at him, my heart rate hitting its stride—wild and fierce. He gave a little nod, like he knew my reaction. Grinning, I stepped out of the car. "Hot."

Saying nothing else, I moved away from the car and up the cement steps leading to the front door of the condo. He just sat idling in his car until I was inside, but I watched through the window when he drove away a few moments after I was secured inside.

My hands were shaking hella bad as I pulled out my cell phone from my backpack and started pounding out a text message to Kayla, but I paused, then deleted before it was done. My feelings for him were my secret.

Dropping the phone back into my pack, I headed for my room, the evening's plans set. Hot shower, fresh clothes, hot meal, set up my GettinHooked.com profile.

CHAPTER 4

I curled up on the family room couch, settling the plate of microwaved pizza rolls across my knees, and watched as Kayla used her dad's new laptop to scroll through the pages that had been added to Gettin-Hooked.com over the weekend. Our site was poppin' off like mad, going from less than a dozen wanna-get-hooked participants to close to forty in just two days.

"How come you haven't done one yet?" Kayla asked, glancing up at me, half her long blond hair in her face. She was sitting on the thick carpet, leaning back against the couch with the laptop on the coffee table.

"I did one." I just hadn't launched it yet, so no one else could see how I'd done up on my profile.

"Don't see it."

"I know. I'm not done." I'm not sure why I was hedging, or why the thought of having my page up twisted my stomach into whack little knots. I put a pizza roll in my mouth, my eyes watering slightly at the heat and making me wish I'd waited until they'd cooled down. Maybe I was straight trippin' for not wanting to talk about my profile, even with my cousin.

Or maybe I was just stalling until Maurice had done his. Once he had his profile up, I'd be able to check out his likes and dislikes. Maybe with a little creative question-answering, I could hook my page up so he'd dig what he read about me.

"Imani?" She touched my knee lightly and slanted her head.

"Hmm?"

"Everything okay?"

The chick knew me too well. I swallowed the bite in my mouth and nodded. "Yeah, girl, I'm aiight." I don't know what was up with me recently, all these crazy like emotions were really getting to me.

"You sure?"

"Fa sheezy."

Kayla stared at me for a bit longer like she was trying to see what was really going down, then shrugged and looked back to the computer. After a quick sec, she turned the monitor toward me. "Did you see these yet?"

There was a dude's page up on the screen. He was hella cute, with a smile that reminded me of Ray J. She waited until I nodded, then hit the next tab bringing up another hottie. "These are Creekside boys." She grinned. "See anything you like?" she teased, adding an eyebrow wiggle.

"They're fine." But they weren't Maurice. They weren't the man I was looking to snag as my prom date. I munched down on another roll.

"There's some hella hot guys at your school, Imani. How come you've never hooked me up before?"

I couldn't help smiling at her, there was so much eagerness shining in her blue eyes. Made me want to laugh, though I was feeling her on the enthusiasm. Our site was going to do exactly what we'd hoped it would. I could just feel it. "You never asked, girl."

She giggled, hitting Next again to bring up the image of another dude from Howard. My school.

"Did you hear that Missy and Jason are talking?"

"Told you she was a bopper."

"Hey!" she said between her laughter as she reached over and smacked my leg. "She's cool."

"Guess Jason thinks so." I winked, then popped another piece of the pizza roll into my mouth.

"You think he'll—" Kayla was interrupted by the chirping of her cell phone. Holding up a *just-a-sec* finger, she flipped it open, turning her attention right quick to the caller rather than the newly hooked couple we'd been talking 'bout.

"In my family room." She flicked through a few

more pages on the computer screen, then reached for the remote and turned down the videos on TV. "Yep, she's here, too. Come over."

Figuring she was talking to one of her girls, I let my thoughts wander back to the bummed-out weekend I'd had, and the short-ass visit with my dad.

He'd flown in Friday mid-morning while I was at school, then spent most of the afternoon at doctor offices with Gram. Later that night, Gram made a rare appearance in the kitchen and fixed these hella smokin' greens that have been my dad's fave since he was a kid and were off the chain.

It was all gravy, hanging Friday night catching up on things with my dad and just chillin' at the crib, something I don't get to do too often with him jetting around the world all the time. We were up late, but then he slept all day Saturday, his body all jacked up because of the whacked-out time zone thing.

Sunday had been cool. It'd rained again, pretty hard, too, so we stayed in and watched movies and grubbed on tons of popcorn. But by evening, I was feeling blue, knowing come morning my dad was blowing our joint to hit the skies again.

And fo' sho', this AM, he dropped me off at school on his way to the airport, giving me some grip just before he drove off. Like a couple C-notes could make up for not having him around enough.

"Hi," I heard Kayla say, yanking me back onto the couch and out of my thoughts. I picked up a pizza roll right quick and plopped it in my mouth to make it look like I was doing something other than sitting like a lump of sludge on my cousin's couch feeling sorry for myself.

Taking a deep breath, I forced away the burn of tears behind my eyes and swallowed the lump of emotion in my throat, then slanted a glance toward the person Kayla had said "hi" to.

Maurice. Snap.

Breathing halted in my chest, burning my lungs.

Heat splashed across my cheeks, and I struggled to chew and swallow the chunk of food I'd just shoved between my lips. I forced a closed-mouth smile. And checked him out. He was dressed hella tight today, in a long-sleeve black Under Armour tee beneath a Raiders' jersey, baggie black FUBU jeans and some clean Jordan 20's.

He looked edible, those full lips of his grinning at me. All casual like, he bent and gave Kayla a hug. "What up, girl?"

After a sec, he angled his body and sat down on the couch between where Kayla sat on the floor leaning against it and where I cuddled in the corner. There wasn't much space, no way enough for his muscular frame, but he sat anyway, his body coming in full contact with mine from the knee up the thigh to our shoulders.

Relaxing into the cushions, he shifted, the hard edges of his body pressing closer, the warmth of him seeping through my clothing. My pulse roared, and I had to turn my face away to keep from inhaling a deep whiff of his yummy scent—all male, Maurice and Curve cologne.

Looking as good as he does, I'd have thought he was frontin' Big Willie style, but his ego was kept in check. He must have known he was hexa fine, but he didn't act like he deserved a little somethin'-somethin' extra because of it.

"Hey, girlie." He nudged me with his elbow gently, then leaned over and plucked the last piece of pizza from the plate with an added wink that caused his dimples to appear. "You been hiding, Imani?"

His voice was low and intimate, like we were alone and knew each other better. Kayla's head swiveled hella fast in my direction, her big, blue eyes wide and questioning.

I shook my head, having a hard concentrating on his question rather than how close he was to me. The way he was touching me. "Marinating."

"Nice." A short chuckle escaped his lips, which then closed around the roll. Realizing I was staring, I busied myself with putting the empty plate on a side table.

We were quiet for a minute, the only sound in the room a soft bass rhythm coming from the video on BET. Beyoncé was blowing. When Maurice finished chewing, he lounged casually on the sofa, seemingly perfectly comfortable in Kayla's home. All smack-dab up against me. Not that I minded, hell no, I was straight digging it.

"You didn't do your page."

Not a question, which means he'd checked. Oh, shit, my heart was racing too frickin' fast. "Not yet."

"Thought we were."

That did it. My cousin was wondering what the hell was going on and I could tell by her expression she was just seconds away from asking. And I didn't want her to, because I wasn't anywhere near ready to answer. Even if I had one.

Forcing a laugh, I replied, "We are." Trying to keep things light and Kayla shut-up, I laughed again and patted his knee. "Did you see all the new pages? Show him, K." Our gazes all locked up, I silently pleaded with her to let it drop. For now. I knew she'd be all over it as soon as we were alone again.

There was a bit of hesitation and her mouth pursed, words just about forming on her lips, but then she shrugged and broke eye contact with me, splitting her attention between the computer and the fine-ass boy sitting beside me.

"Peep all these." She moved to the *girls'* pages, then started clicking the mouse through each profile, giving Maurice a quick second to look at each.

"More added."

"Yup. Hey, Imani, two more added while we sat here."

"Boys or girls?" I asked.

"Girls."

Gritting my teeth, I squeezed my lids closed for a brief moment, hoping like hell the girls weren't pretty. Or at least not the kind of goodies Maurice was into.

Laughter filled the room. One of the Creekside girls was showing a hella lot of skin in her pictures. "That duck looks like a ho."

Kayla laughed. "No kidding. Look at these shots." She clicked on some of the girl's other photos.

"This yours?" Maurice asked, his fingers draping across my thigh as he swooped my cell phone from my lap.

I nodded, but tried to keep my focus on my cousin as she showed us the profile of the second newly added wanna-prom-date girl. From the corner of my eye, I could see Maurice open my phone.

What was he doing? I wondered, as his thumb moved through files, his gaze shifting from the tiny screen to the monitor and pages on my uncle's computer. What was he doing? Reading text messages? All my recent messages played out in my mind, hoping there wasn't anything incriminating. There shouldn't be. My feelings for him were still on the down low. Except for whatever Kayla suspected was going on. Not that I knew.

But I didn't think he was reading my messages anyway, his thumb was moving through the pages too quickly. Was he checking numbers? Seeing who I had listed in my phone book? Was he curious if I had a lot of guys?

Kayla was saying something else, but I wasn't even sure she was speaking English let alone knew what she was saying, even though I kept my gaze steady in her direction.

The cool, hard plastic of my phone was tucked into my palm, and Maurice's strong hands eased my fingers closed around it. Glancing up, I looked into his dark eyes, then arched a brow at him.

He chuckled. "Programmed my number," he answered, reading my look.

My lips moved, but my throat was tight and dry and no real sound came out. "Thanks."

He nodded.

Kayla had stopped talking and was openly staring at us again.

Wetting my lips, I took a couple shallow breaths, trying to slow the thumpin'-bumpin' beat of my heart. My hands shook, and not wanting Maurice to feel, I pulled away from him, scrambling to my feet.

"I've got to jet, K. Tons of homework." I grabbed my pack from the floor and yanked it over a shoulder.

"Wanna ride?" Maurice and Kayla asked at the same

time. My cousin was looking at me all puzzled like. He was about to stand.

"Nah. I'll walk." There were days—and this was one of 'em—that I needed the time alone to shift through things in my head. I'd be wet by the time I made it home; the rain was still coming down lightly. But the cool air and damp conditions were exactly what I needed.

"I'll text you," I said to Kayla, but I couldn't even look her in the eye. "You, too?" I lifted my phone and arched a brow at him again. He'd understood both times, because he grinned and nodded.

Turning away, I left the family room, moving away from the sound of Akon and Snoop's latest. I was about in the kitchen, the way I always came and went from their house, when I heard my auntie talking. It took me a sec to realize she was talking on the phone and not to me.

Her words made me falter, then flatten my back against the wall, the baby hairs at the nape of my neck prickling.

"She's here now," my auntie said softly. After a pause she added, "Don't you want to know about her?"

She shook her head, her back to me, and I could tell by the way her shoulders moved that she let out a deep sigh.

"Well, okay. Talk to you soon." She hung up the phone and let it drop onto the tile counter with a thunk, before she moved toward the stove.

But I stayed where I was, near the kitchen door, my back against the wall and my knees shaking so badly, I doubt I coulda walked right away. Who'd been on the phone? I couldn't help wondering. Something nagged at me. Something made breathing difficult and left me confused and completely depleted of energy.

To hell with the winter weather doing me good. I shoulda told Maurice I wanted that ride home. Wedging my bottom lip between my teeth, I pushed from the wall, the movement attracting my auntie's attention.

She glanced over her shoulder at me. "Oh, sweetie, I didn't see you there."

"Just headed home," I lied, unwilling to confess how whack I'd been to listen in on the ending to her conversation.

"It's nasty outside. Let me give you a ride." She looked at me again, then quickly back at the pot on the stove. But not so quickly that I didn't see the shimmer of guilt in eyes the same shade of blue as Kayla's.

I shifted my backpack from one shoulder, sliding in the second arm. "I'll just walk." And then I was across the room and out the slider door, the blast of wind and rain stinging my face. The relief intense.

Damn near running by the time I hit the street, I was hella trippin' over what had happened in there. First Maurice sitting all up on me, then putting his number in my phone, then my auntie talking on the phone.

Shit, it coulda been *anyone* on the other end of the line. Coulda been *about* anyone. But I couldn't help the twisting of my gut, the nagging suspicion that it wasn't just anyone, it was my mom.

CHAPTER 5

Ten days ago all anyone talked about was MySpace. Who they were talking to, who they'd met, who was fine, who was leavin' crazy-ass comments on whose page. Ten days ago, I spent whack hours updating my profile, changing the songs and videos, uploading silly pictures from my digital camera.

Ten days ago, I've got to admit, MySpace was the shit. But that was before GettinHooked.com blew up our zip code.

Now MySpace was hardly mentioned at all, and I heard nothing but buzz over our Web site and the whole prom date hook-up thang. My girls were all over this, hyped on the chance to check out the dudes at Creekside.

And I was hearing 'bout it every chance they got, between classes, during lunch, after school, texts on my cell. It was gravity, though, because I was straight digging the attention. Cool with being the one all the

Howard fellas went to when they wanted to know about my cousin and her friends.

GettinHooked.com was bubbling and Kayla and I were in the middle of it.

The talk about our hook-up system was constant. Even now, during my American Government class library time, I could hear some girls whispering a few tables over. Their voices carried in the hushed quiet of study.

Not my friends really, but a couple of beezies who gave up their goodies way too easy. Not that I really had a problem with these girls. Nah, we were cool. I just don't get down to the nasty the way they do.

Creekside boys were going to be thankin' me, I thought, biting my bottom lip to keep from laughing. Yanking up my hoodie, I focused on the book spread-eagle on the table in front of me. But even in the bright overhead lighting, the words mingled and fuzzed, my thoughts drifting ahead toward prom, and wondering if GettinHooked would work out the way I'd planned it to.

Like everyone else, I was obsessed with the Web site.

"Dayum," one girl said, her voice squealing as she drew out the *m*. "Did you peep the new guys' profiles?"

There was some muffled laughter. "Hella fine."

I wasn't really listening, but I could still hear most of their hushed words. Knew exactly what they were talking about.

"I'ma get me some of that one boy."

"Who?"

Yeah, who? I wondered, adjusting my hoodie so I could angle my eyes toward Chelsea and Brie, the two girls talking, though I wasn't sure which of them had commented on wanting one of the Creekside hotties.

But right as I looked over, Brie glanced my way and caught my eye. And smiled, kind of faulty, but whatever. I've known Brie since second grade when we ended up in the same class. Chelsea moved here a couple years back, from L.A., and brought some Southern Cali snob attitude with her, up here near The Bay.

Though we were cool, we weren't exactly friends, either, as we never hung at the same places, and I know these chicks wouldn't have given a damn about me if it weren't for my Web site.

Brie broke eye contact first, glancing to Chelsea and whispering something. A few seconds later, they were gathering their stuff and grabbing their backpacks to move over to the table where I was sitting.

"Hey girl, that shit you hooked up is hella clean," Brie said, sliding into the plastic chair next to mine.

Chelsea snapped her fingers before jabbing her hands to her popped-out hip. "Off the heezy."

"Thanks."

"You know all those dudes?"

I shook my head. "The Creekside guys?" After they both nodded, I went on. "Nah, only some of 'em. They're mostly Kayla's peeps."

"Fo sheedo?" Chelsea mumbled.

There was some sarcasm in her tone and I straight wanted to call her on it, but decided it best to let it go. Narrowing my eyes, I glared at her for sec, until the beotch backed down and plopped her ass into another chair.

For real? Like I was holding some info back. Totally wasn't feeling her attitude. If I'd known all those fellas the way I wanted to know one, they'd never even be asking. I'd have found another way to be with my boo.

"You know some, though, right?" Brie must have been the one who'd been wanting to get her some of. She was crazy insistent.

"I guess."

"There's a new guy. You know 'im?"

Shrugging, I thought over the guys who'd added last night. I'd gotten up late this morning, sleeping through my alarm until Gram had finally come in and shook my ass awake. That happens sometimes when I stay up till the A.M.s texting and marinatin'. And oversleeping had cost me a quick check of the site this morning.

GettinHooked.com now had more than two hundred users and profiles. And more adding all the damn time. No way was I going to know what boy she was talking 'bout.

"How new?" I asked, because at least that'd help narrow it down.

"This morning."

Fricking figures.

Chelsea smacked Brie's upper arm. "He is *fiiinnne!* My girl wants him bad."

We all laughed, attracting glances from other students in the library. Brie did seem a little desperate. He must be hexa sexi. Pulling my cell from my pocket right quick, I glanced at the time just to see how much longer until I could blow this joint and get online. Check out who they were talking about for myself.

About twenty minutes. "I haven't looked at the new profiles yet. What's his name?"

"Maurice something. I can't remember brotha's last name."

A loud pounding started behind my ears and it took me a minute to figure out that it was my pulse bumping like bass drums. Maurice. *My Maurice.* Doing everything I could to look like I was chill, I struggled to breathe, but my lungs were all seized up and burning.

If they meant *my* Maurice, not that he was really mine—yet—that'd mean that he'd gone ahead and set up his profile like he said he was going to. Or maybe I was tripping. Last I checked he didn't have a page yet, and there could be more than one Maurice at Creekside. Shit, as far as I know there could be a dozen.

"Simms?" My voice cracked. I could hear it, but hoped like mad neither Chelsea nor Brie noticed. And hoped like hell she said no.

Brie licked her lips. "Simms. Yeah, that him. Maurice Simms." Fanning her face, she lounged back in her stiff plastic seat. "That boy smokin' enough to get some of my treats."

Behind my eyes started to sting, and I knew that meant the possibility of tears. Blinking, I pushed the liquid away. Hell no, I wasn't crying over a boy.

Not even Maurice Simms.

When my I was little, I used to cry over not having a momma. Gram would hold me, my cheek pressed against her shoulder as she stroked my soft, kinky hair. "You can cry over your momma, Imani," she'd whispered, "but don't never, ever cry 'bout a boy." Gram's words rang loudly in my conscience now.

Swallowing twice, I tried to clear the lump in my dry throat, to shove away the nausea churning in my gut. I'd done this all for him; sold Kayla on the idea, spent enough homework hours building our site that my grades could suffer, dismissed checking out other boys. I'd done this all for the chance to have a prom night to remember.

For the chance to be with Maurice.

Now I could lose the chance because some trick offering up easily opened thighs was stalking his fine ass. Bopper, the girl was fo sho a bopper. Only a ho would be offering up sex before she'd even met the guy.

"...him a message. See if he wants to hook up."

Getting my tripping behind together, I pulled my attention back to the conversation. I'd missed what Brie had been saying, only catching the tail end.

"Girl, shoot, if he don't want none of you, I'll take 'im," Chelsea said, making a show of licking her lips.

Lawdy, I wanted out of here now. Away from the table, away from the leg-spreading bendas, out of the library. Done with the school day. I needed to check Maurice's profile, and I needed to straight get ahold of Kayla and find out...I paused and took a deep breath as reality seeped in.

Find out what from Kayla? She didn't even know I had it bad for the brotha who lived across the street. And even though he'd driven me home and put his number in my phone didn't mean anything more than he was a nice guy. Sure didn't mean he was into me.

I had no claim, so if he wanted to respond to the GettinHooked messages that were sure to flood his box, that was on him.

"Imani, did you hear Mikey Harper and that one Creekside girl, Shay Kline, hooked up already?" Chelsea asked.

"I knew they were messaging. Whatcha mean by hooked up?"

Brie giggled. "Doing the do."

"How do you know?" I'd lost it, really. What was I doing sitting here gossiping with a couple of beezies? What I needed to do was get my American Government done right quick so I could spend the rest of the night matching up my profile to Maurice's, just on the slight chance he'd pass up the offer of easy booty for me.

"Saw 'em at Walgreens buying condoms."

My eyes got all wide in surprise. "Really?" Dayum... I guess GettinHooked was no joke. I laughed, even as I shook my head. "Guess my site works."

Through broken giggles, Brie said, "Fa' sheezy, girl."

"How come you don't have a page?" Chelsea was watching me all close, her mouth twisted into a smirk.

Something was up with the girl today, the attitude brimming right up to her eyeballs. She could be down-right nasty to folks she didn't like, and I knew this. Still, I wasn't having it. She came to my table and she wanted on my site, then she best come at me with some respect.

Glaring back at her, I waited for her to ask again or make something of it. All bluster, I guess, because for the second time in ten minutes, she dropped the tone and checked her attitude.

She shrugged, then asked again a little more nicely. "You going to do a page, Imani?"

Um, yeah, tonight…or, shoot, right after school. "I'm getting around to it." Some shuffling across the room caught my attention and I realized that other students were gathering their things and zipping up their packs. That had to mean the clock was 'bout to spring us from school. "I'm gravy, though, and not worried about it," I said casually, closing the book and leaning over to get my bag.

"Who you want to go to prom with?" Brie asked. "You had to have some dude in mind when you started this mess, didn't you?"

Shiieet, this chick was smarter than I gave her ho ass credit for. Damn straight, I knew who I wanted— always had, but no way was I going to tell her that she wanted the same hottie I did. No way was I going to let her think we were in competition.

My heart had started thumping again, along with a tingle of apprehension that was working its way down my spine. "Don't know." *A lie.* Standing and shrugging my pack over my shoulder, I reached into the side pocket, then fit my stunnas over my eyes. "Haven't checked all the profiles yet." The truth, but I intended to as soon as I got my butt in front of my computer.

The bell rang. Voices rose around us, and the flow of movement went eagerly toward the door as the rest of the students hustled out.

"I'm out," I said, flashing Chelsea and Brie a peace

sign, then turned and quit the library before they said anything else.

Hard to believe it was Friday already, nearly a week since my dad had come and gone again, and a few more days before he was landing in The Bay again. At least that meant that I'd be free tonight and tomorrow, unlike last weekend.

I walked along beneath the building overhang, but then reached for my umbrella and snapped it open as I moved on, away from school and toward home. The steady drizzle still hadn't let up none, but at least it wasn't all that cold.

A few other kids walked along around me, some drifting off in directions, giving a quick wave or shout-out goodbye. I returned the see-ya's, but didn't slow, too dang eager to get home and see the profile fine-ass Maurice put up.

Time to do what I could to make my own appealing, more appealing than the flood of other pigeons he was no doubt about to get. I knew Maurice was hot. Knew he was fun postin' with. Knew he was hella nice. Time now to see what kind of guy he really was. Guess I'd soon find out.

CHAPTER 6

I thumbed into my cell, ? up 4 2nite, then hit the button to send the text to Kayla. I'd been home a few hours, but pretty much hadn't done much besides stare at Maurice's profile on GettinHooked.com. Damn— the boy is fine. It was cool looking through the profile lists of his likes and dislikes, and I found myself smiling a few times, really digging this guy.

It was kind of weird having looked at him all this time, passing by the cutie on my way to Kayla's, peeping him every chance I got, and knowing he was hot, knowing that I was down with what I saw. But it was totally different now, reading about him and realizing this was a dude I could like. I mean hella like. A lot.

I'd changed out of my damp jeans when I landed in the condo, and pulled on some warm sweats, then yanked my mad curls into a band at the back of my head, knowing they were going to frizz since they'd gotten wet. If I was going out with Kayla tonight I'd have to totally redo my hair.

Shoving the cell into my pocket while I waited for her to respond, I headed to Gram's room. I hadn't talked to her much since I'd gotten home and wanted to make sure she had everything she needed before I went out for the night.

Pale light seeped out her half-opened door, not just from the TV but from a small table lamp. That was kind of weird, considering I hardly ever saw the light on because it bothers her eyes. Leaning around the door, I looked inside and saw her sitting her favorite recliner, rocking slowly before the news.

"Hi, Gram," I said, moving into her room.

She swiveled the chair, turning toward me, shifting something on her lap, then sliding it beneath an oversize book. "What is it, baby?"

My attention was fixed on the fact that she seemed to be hiding whatever it was that she'd been looking at. And I couldn't help wondering why. "Just wanted to see how you're doing, Gram." Though I answered, I couldn't get my thoughts from lingering on what was now covered by the pages of her book.

"I'm good, girl. Don't you be worrying yourself about me, child."

But her voice sounded sad, a little more distant than

usual. Maybe she was looking at pictures of my granddad. I've seen her doing that a bunch before, and it always seemed to bring on this mood. Must be it, I decided, not wanting to press her much about it.

Moving farther into her room, I sat down on the edge of her bed so we could talk for a bit before I hit the town. Okay, not so much the town, but maybe a party or movie or *something* other than staying home on a Friday night. "Has daddy called?"

She glanced slowly at the phone, the look of sadness somehow overshadowed by the darker image of guilt. What she had to feel guilty about, I couldn't guess. She couldn't change the fact that my dad worked for the airlines and spent most of his time in the sky. Gram sure as hell wasn't responsible for the fact that my momma couldn't deal with being a momma and skipped out on me before I'd formed any real memories of her.

Gram shifted her gaze back to me, looking me straight in the face. "No, Imani, he hasn't. Not since Wednesday night."

"He must be busy." I knew he was, because I knew deep in my heart if he wasn't he'd have called me. But even knowing it doesn't help ease the ache sometimes. "He'll be home this week, still?"

"Baby, I'm sure he will." Her voice cracked as she spoke, and the strange mix of sadness and guilt clouded the sweetness of her words. Gram shifted forward, reaching to take my hand. She squeezed gently, the touch soft but firm, always the way of her loving.

Clamping my lids closed, I willed away the flow of tears, something about Gram's mood dragging on me. Swiping my free hand across my cheek to catch the lone escapee droplet that seeped past my lashes, I took a couple of breaths, then opened my eyes to see Gram looking me in the face.

"Is it something else, Imani?" she asked.

"Nah, just miss him, is all." Reassuring her nothing else was popping off in my life, I leaned toward her to give her a hug right quick, but when I put my arms around her the book shifted on her lap and I caught the corner of a picture.

Of me. My most recent school photo, the corner tucked into an envelope, a handwritten address mostly still hidden beneath the hardcover of the book. My gram's handwriting, telling me she was sending it out.

Oh, lawdy, my chest hurt bad, as my heart stopped beating for a sec. And my breath caught in my lungs as some strange pressure tightened around my stomach. Who was Gram sending a picture of me to? Some long hidden place in my soul gave a shout-out, that maybe— just maybe—she was sending a picture to my momma.

I had to bounce. Had to step out of her room, step the hell out of our condo before I pressed her about it. Gram wouldn't do that to me. She wouldn't. I had to keep on believing that, and even with the little nagging doubt, I sure wasn't ready to look for an answer right now. Maybe not ever. My momma left me, I told myself. I didn't need to be fussing 'bout it at all. It was her loss.

Straightening away from Gram, I smoothed my damp palms across my thighs just as my cell vibrated in my pocket. "I'm going out tonight, Gram. You all right if I stay at Kayla's?"

"I'm grown, Imani. I know how to take care of myself." The resentment I always heard from her when I spent time with my momma's family was back, replacing the other weirdness.

"I know." I kissed her cheek, then looked at the door so I wouldn't stare at the corner of my picture poking out of its hiding place on her lap.

"You be careful, girl."

"I will."

"Don't be getting in no trouble, you hear?"

"Fo' sho', Gram, I'm not about trouble," I teased by adding a wink, then scooted right quick out of the way as she swatted playfully at my butt. Nope, I wasn't looking for trouble tonight, unless you called hooking up with Maurice trouble. I called it fun.

Assuming, of course, that Kayla and I ended up marinating at the same place he was chillin' tonight. Hopefully my girl had the inside track of where we'd find him tonight, though I'd have to be on the down low about peeping the info since she didn't know I was feelin' the boy.

"I'll let you know when I'm out."

"All right, baby."

Forcing a smile, I left her room, closing the door all the way this time, then fiddling in my pocket for my cell.

Dwn 4 a prty?, glared at me from the small, dark screen. Hell, yeah, I could be down for a party, and if it was Kayla's crew, there was a good chance my boy would be there, too. Grinning, I thumbed in my yep, then headed to my room to pick out something hella bangin' to wear.

As I sorted through my Apple Bottoms jeans and my saucy tops, I thought about calling Kayla and trying to find out more about the party. Was it a kickback or a house party? Was Moms and Pops out of town, 'cause that fa sheezy would change up the scene, and maybe how I'd want to dress. Although, hoping Maurice was there, dress to impress would be the code for the night.

Gt U in 45, bleeped a message onto my cell, telling me that Kayla and I wouldn't be alone tonight and one of her girls most likely would be driving. With only forty-five minutes until they came to get me, I knew I had to pick up my getting-ready pace.

Tossing a couple hella cute outfits on the bed, I

headed for the bathroom and plugged in my flatiron, knowing I was going to have to redo most of my hair since it'd gotten wet and the kink was coming out in a fierce way. It was while I was waiting for the flatiron to heat up that my mind kept wondering, drifting back and forth between Maurice and my picture hidden on my Gram's lap.

Part of me wanted to blow off Kayla, party, Maurice, going out. That part wanted to march back into my gram's room and demand to know what the hell that picture was all about. I knew, I really knew, there was something to it. And as much as I wanted to dismiss it no matter what Gram was hiding, relying on the excuse that I didn't give a shit, that same part kept nagging me 'bout it.

And then, how could I blow off the chance to spend the night at a party with Maurice? Even if that picture had something to do with my momma, as I suspected, hell no, my momma wasn't worth skipping out on the guy I wanted. Wasn't worth the time my head was fussing over it.

On the here and now relationship I was hinting at getting is where my mind belonged. On Maurice, with his caramel skin and warm, friendly eyes. With his cheeks cut with dimples, and his sculpted bod, that did silly things to my insides when we touched.

Combing through a chunk of hair, I clamped the

iron on it, then pulled it straight, repeating the process until my hair was tamed and back into pre-rain condition. I didn't bother with makeup much, but had a serious thing for lipgloss. Applying my favorite, I headed back to my room to dress.

Not sure which of the outfits to choose, I dialed my cousin's cell real quick.

"What up, girl?" she answered.

"Hey, K. Kickback casual, or sexy dance-ware?"

She giggled across the line. "Sexy dance-ware, Imani."

I laughed at her tone. "Oh, it's like that?"

"Yup." She mumbled something to someone else before coming back on the phone. "You 'bout ready?"

"Gimme ten minutes."

"Sure thing, girl. See you in ten."

The line went dead, so I clicked my cell shut, then hustled to pull on some low-rise jeans, a pink thin-strapped short top, and some matching K-Swiss sneakers. Once dressed, I smeared a shimmering, sweet-scented lotion across my skin, made sure my gloss was glimmering and found a puffy jacket.

With just a few minutes to spare, I shoved the sweats I'd been wearing and a change of clothes into my pack, and quit my room.

I knocked once on Gram's door, then stood there waiting for her to call me in. Normally I'd have just knocked then stuck my head inside, but I wanted to give her time to put those pictures of me away if she still had 'em out. I couldn't deal with this now. I had other things to trip on.

Not only was I trying to arrange my own thang, but I had messages from a grip of guys and girls from Howard and Creekside who were all looking for hookups and prom dates.

"Yeah, baby?" I heard Gram say.

Opening the door just enough for me to peek in, I leaned inside and said, "Gram, I'm out. I'll be back tomorrow." I waited for her sour face, the one she always gets when she knows I'm going to my cousin's. I only saw a slight glimpse of it, which was kind of weird, but I wasn't going to twiddle on it.

"Don't be out too late, Imani. You know the only things open after two are bars and legs, and you don't belong doing neither."

I shook my head, stunned by her rebuke. Gram warned about boys. That was standard. This is the first time the warning got specific—and kind of crude. Gram was off her rocker, acting hexa strange tonight.

My throat feeling a little tight, I swallowed before responded. "We'll be back to Kayla's before two, Gram."

"Good girl."

"Hey, Gram?" I glanced at her, catching her eyes. The moment held there, suspended and stretched.

"Yeah, baby?"

The words were there, all lingering in my throat, curling and taking shape in my mouth, clinging desperately to my tongue. The questions were busting to come out, but I couldn't let them.

Silence seeped across the room causing the fine little baby hairs on the back of my neck to stand up and a shiver to creep down my spine. The quiet tension continued, only to be interrupted by the buzz of my cell, the call from Kayla letting me know they were here.

I hesitated shutting it off, not breaking eye contact, knowing now it was just a matter of time before I knew what was up, and pretty damn sure I didn't want to.

"Go ahead, Imani. They're waiting on you."

I nodded, then looked away. "Night, Gram."

"Night, baby."

Holding tight on to my pack, I headed out the door. Time to forget the home-side drama. Time for boostin' mine.

CHAPTER 7

Kayla's friend, Dasia, drove her older brother's Impala with twenty-inch gold rims, and a tight paint job. The perfect ride to be creepin' up to parties in, and Dasia knew how to swing and dip it.

Giggling hard as she smashed the brake and flung the ride to the curb and into Park, it took the three of us a minute to quit laughing before we left the car, straightening our clothes, messing with our hair, and double-checking the gloss on our lips.

The night was dark and damp, but at least the drizzle had quit. Low clouds hovered, blocking out any light we may have gotten from the moon. The streetlight at the corner blinked in and out—mostly out—and didn't do much to brighten up the drive.

The party had to be bumpin' because the streets around the alley were packed with cars and we'd had to park around the corner and a couple of courts over before we found a spot. We hadn't walked far, though, when the thumping of bass broke into the night's silence.

A little farther and we started seeing others heading toward the party. Strangers to me, but Kayla and Dasia's peeps. They called out "hi," a couple of times, waved a few more.

"This is gonna be hexa fun," Kayla commented, snapping her fingers and swiveling her hip to the side.

Dasia laughed, copying her finger snapping and hip movement. "Fa shizzle."

"You think there'll be folkies I know?"

"You know me," Dasia said, slinging her arm around my shoulder.

"True." I glanced at Dasia. She was strikingly different than Kayla, her dark skin and cornrowed hair was contrasted by Kayla's creamy complexion and long blond waves. I'd known her for a couple of years, and we'd hung out plenty, since she was Kayla's girl. She was cool people, too, fun and sincere. We got along really well.

"Besides, girl—" Kayla cut in "—what's it matter if you know anyone? Look at you. All the fellas will be on ya in a minute. Yadadamean, yadadamean?"

Dasia and I looked at each other again, then both at Kayla before we cracked up. *Yadadamean* coming from her sounded hella funny, and we knew she'd added it for the silly effect.

"Yeah, girlie, I'm feelin' ya." I knew I looked good— nothing wrong with being confident. And I knew I never had a problem pulling boys. But there was only one dude I was wanting up on me tonight. And if there hadn't been a prob getting his attention, I wouldn't have been trippin' about my lack of a prom date. I'd have had one. Him.

I took a deep breath, then let it out slowly. "I'm feelin' ya, K," I said softly, then did a little Vanna White impression down my body, "but if so many dudes are wanting some of this, how come I need Gettin-Hooked.com to get a prom date?"

"You told me why. You've known the boys at your school too long."

"I guess." My mood was deflated a little.

"Girlie, GettinHooked.com is off the chain. How'd you think of it?" Dasia asked.

I shrugged, but couldn't help the proud grin. "I've been going to school with the same dudes since kinder-garten. They're tired and played out as boyfriend material for me." I winked. "But Creekside fellas are fresh meat for me, same for you and Howard."

"Yup." Dasia flicked open her ringing cell as she answered.

"I was updating MySpace and realized we needed something like that, but locals, girlfriend, so hook-ups could happen."

"That house," Kayla said, pointing into a cul-de-sac and the house what had music pumping out and kids flowing in.

We turned toward it and kept walking and Kayla kept talking. "And it's jumping off. We have more than two hundred pages now, and the hook-ups are happening. Hella people are talkin' now."

"I'ma find me a boy," Dasia said, her voice drowning out into the rhythm and raps as we entered the house.

It was shaded inside, just some low lighting in the back end of the front room. The second we stepped in the door I could smell the scent of Henny, boody-funk of folks dancing too hard and the lingering fragrance of Mary Jane.

Fo' sho', the parents had to be out of town or something, because this was the sort of pallay that woulda been shut down otherwise.

A few more steps in and Dasia disappeared into the crowd, hugging people as she moved away, shaking her ass with each step, following the rolling beat.

Kayla grabbed my hand, pulling me a bit to the side. "Dayum," she shouted over the roar of the music and hype of her friends. She hugged a few guys—cute ones, but nothing special—intro'd me right quick, then started talking to them, the words lost to me in the volume of the party.

Taking on the rhythm, I started flowing with it,

rocking beside Kayla as she laughed at something one of the dudes had said. I knew one of them was talking 'bout me. I could feel the eyeballs, could hear the murmur of their voices and knew Kayla's matchmaking techniques.

But I was using the movement of my dance as a disguise to look around the room, shifting so I could get peeks over bobbing heads and around grinding asses. My cousin could try all the fixin' up she wanted, but I was looking for one guy.

And I found him.

Maurice stood out, taller than many of the dudes there, his shoulders broader. He was dancing, his body doing the same sort of hyphie movements I'd seen when he was mowing the lawn.

My pulse picked up, and I knew I was staring. And smiling. Thinking 'bout my approach and getting prepped to dance, I slid off my jacket. Body heat would keep me plenty warm enough.

"Where should we dump these?"

One of the guys Kayla was talking to whistled between his teeth. "Nice. A dime girl. Lemme holla atcha."

Kayla smacked his upper arm, but she was grinning wide. She slanted her head toward a chair no one was sitting in. "Let's put 'em over there. I'll keep an eye."

I nodded and handed off my jacket, my attention returning right quick to Maurice.

"—with your cousin," I heard the guy saying something to Kayla, trying to get a hook-up with me, I'm sure. It was the outfit, the dress to impress had done the trick, I thought with a smile.

Not trying to diss, but I wasn't interested, so I pretty much ignored him. "I'm gonna dance," I said to Kayla as I started to move away.

Ducking and dodging around the craziness of the dance floor, I'd only gotten halfway across the room, smack in the middle of a mob of folkies getting their grooves on, when I stopped dead in my tracks.

Maurice wasn't alone.

He was now grinding with a girl, and I stood there, getting whacked into and bounced around, just staring. Unable to move. Hell, hardly able to breathe.

Standing like a statue, frozen in my K-Swiss, and Maurice lifted his eyes, his gaze landing smack on me and sticking. His expression was unreadable, the warmth of his smiling eyes missing from his stare.

And dammit, but I felt my own well up, and tears gather on my lashes. I could only hope he was far enough away and the room dim enough that he didn't notice. I tried to push them back, to keep them from falling, and I'm pretty sure it worked, but I couldn't be sure because I couldn't think.

The music faded, one song ending and the pause before the next deafening. The second ticked by gingerly before the next song bumped from the speakers, and still we looked into each other's eyes.

Then the girl rubbed up against him, stroked her hand across his chest, turned and followed the direction of his stare. I knew the moment she saw me, shock sending a shiver down my spine.

I knew the beezy—Brie. Brie, the bopper, who'd be spreading her legs for Maurice tonight, if he wanted it.

I glanced away from her right quick, looking Maurice in his still-expressionless eyes. I glared just for a sec, then somehow found the will to turn and walk away, slipping between a couple of people so he couldn't see me anymore.

My chest was aching, something bitter flooded through my blood and churned painfully in my gut. Moving across the room, I found a narrow piece of unoccupied wall and leaned my back against it, a little freaked that my knees might not hold.

I couldn't really go back over to Kayla, because really, what was I supposed to say? I wanted your neighbor but I was too cowardly to tell him, so I came up with a scheme to get him, only it backfired on my ass and he ended up with an easy sleazy ho.

Unable to help it, I glanced toward him, my spot obscured by the crowd and I didn't think he'd be able to see me. But Brie could. She was hella muggin' me, like I was some sort of threat.

I scoffed. I wasn't offering what she was, and Maurice was a dude. Most don't give up the sure thing for something they're not getting yet.

Turning away, I closed my eyes and exhaled a couple of times. As I evened my breathing, my mind skipped back to the times I'd hung with him, the ride home in the rain, the digits he'd put in my phone, the interest in when I was putting up my GettinHooked profile.

I'd thought maybe. But what did I really know 'bout him? Sure thing, I'd read his profile lists and dug him. More than his fine-ass looks. But I wasn't into playas, and didn't do second best. If he was the kind of boy who went for girls like her, forget him then, I was through.

Gathering my scruff, I shoved off the wall and made my way back to where I'd left Kayla, hoping the guy who'd been interested was still hanging round. He was. I moved right up next to him, close enough for him to catch a whiff of sweet-scented lotion, close enough for him to catch a glimpse down my saucy top.

Putting my hand softly on his arm, I leaned a little closer, then whispered, "Dance with me?" so just he could hear. Yeah, I was playing tease, but I needed to. I needed his attention because my confidence was tweaked by Maurice choosing a bootch over me.

"Fo' sho', little momma," he said, bending to put his arms low around my back, then moving us farther into the room and away from the group Kayla was chilling with.

Putting my arms around his shoulders, I let him grind some, allowing the bass and melody to lead our movements. The second he bent his head and started softly singing the words of the song, I knew the boy was hella faded, his breath straight reeking from tippin' back a bottle.

I laughed, his words slurred, his body laxed and just tried to get into dancing and forget about the glare burning on my back. It was hexxa strange the way I could tell the difference between when Brie was staring uglies and when Maurice was watching. But I just knew.

And knowing that it was Maurice's eyes landing on me, I snuggled closer to my dance partner. Hell, Kayla had introed us, but I hadn't even bothered to remember his name, too overly focused on the hottie I was trying to zero from my thoughts. And from my heart.

And though I couldn't see him, I knew the moment Maurice looked away, the wash of cold across my skin unmistakable. I knew I was finished with him. If Brie wanted him, she could have him. But as the cold trickled down my back, I yearned for the return of his heat.

"Hey," Kayla said, yanking me back into the moment as she shoved my jacket at me. "A neighbor called the popos. Time to bounce."

I stepped away from the cutie, shrugging on my jacket.

"Lemme roll with y'all," he said.

"Nah, maybe another time." With an added wink I let the tease sink in, then fell into step with Kayla as we headed for the door. Dasia caught up with us right as we stepped outside, and the three of us jogged to the end of the court, then disappeared into the moonless night before the twirl of red and blue arrived.

I could only hope now that Maurice wasn't parked anywhere near where we'd left our ride. I didn't want to see him again tonight.

Maybe never again.

CHAPTER 8

WRAPPING my hands around the warm paper cup, I cuddled up next to Kayla, tucking my feet beneath me on those comfy little sofas they have in Starbucks' lobbies, and leaned my head on her shoulder. Dasia had slept over at Kayla's, too, and we'd been up hella late, laughing, gossiping and messing with GettinHooked.com.

But I was tired now, not having slept well after we'd finally knocked out for the night. Every time I closed my eyes; I could see Maurice's, the way we'd looked at each other and the way he'd stared me down when I was dancing with Darian.

Kayla and Dasia had filled me in all about him as soon as we'd skipped out before the cops arrived.

Holding back a yawn, I closed my eyes, allowing the warmth of the latte to seep up my arms, and the soft murmuring words of Kayla and Dasia to loll me into my own thoughts, and memories of the evening before.

Darian Gage. Junior at Creekside. Played basketball and football for the school. Kayla, Dasia and I had spent about an hour going over his GettinHooked profile, and from what I could peep about the boy, we actually had a lot in common. I could get into him, consider him as prom-date material, even. Except he had a little bit of a rep as being a playa.

Still, he was hella fine. Not Maurice hottie status, but fo' real, few compared. As I'd lain there, curled into the oversize beanbag chair, trying to sleep, I kept thinking about these two dudes. The one I'd wanted and the one who wanted me.

I'd kept remembering the way Brie had been touching Maurice, the way he'd been grinding with her, enjoying the way she moved against him. And I'd kept wondering if they were hooking up right then, as I was restless on a beanbag on my cousin's room.

Then there was Darian, with his muscular body and obvious interest in me. I could tell; we'd danced hexa close. I felt a little guilty about the way I'd teased the poor guy, used him actually to make Maurice jealous. Or at least let him know I wasn't hung up or bothered by seeing him with another girl.

"I signed up." A new girl's voice entered the mumbled words of my cousin and friend, pulling me from my drowsy closed-eyes musings.

Lifting my lids, I checked out the newcomer, a chick

I didn't know. Must have been one of Kayla's Creek-side classmates, I decided, allowing my lids to flutter closed again, deciding I'd rather just listen than take part in the conversation.

"Cool. You digging it?" Kayla's voice. I knew it well.

"Oh, yeah, girl. I already started talking to someone. Jonathan Brown. You know him?"

I did. He was in my chemistry class. I didn't say anything though, because I didn't know he'd made a profile page. He already had a girlfriend.

"We went to the movies last night."

Shit. Okaaay, I hadn't really thought of the fact that some folkies may use this as a way to double up on who they'd already got. I think I'd have said something to Jonathan had I seen his profile up there, but there was getting to be so many it was hard to keep up.

Our number of profiles had jumped again, nearly reaching five frickin' hundred now. We'd been around for two weeks. My girls were all over this. Some had even made prom date commitments already. Things were bouncing off just as I'd hoped they would. Better. Except for me. Maurice was out of the picture, but at least I had a possible backup in Darian.

Dasia giggled. "You have fun, Leza?"

"Oh, my God, yes!" She laughed. "He's fiiinnnee."

"I know I am, girlie." A new voice. A guy. I opened my eyes to see who'd just walked up on us.

Darian. Aww lawdy, I was wearing baggie sweats, had my hair in a pony and most of my lip gloss was lingering on the rim of my coffee cup.

"Hey, Darian," Dasia and Kayla said in unison, Kayla discreetly pinching me on the side.

"What up?" He nodded at them, but was looking right at me, a smile threatening on his lips.

"Hi," I whispered. My voice cracked, sounding like I'd just woken up.

"Can I talk atcha for a sec?"

My face heated like crazy, and I wondered if Darian and my girls could see the pink rising on my cheeks. My heart rate kicked up some, more about the situation than Darian, though. "Fa sheezy."

"In private?"

Oh, snap, it was like that? "Sure." I straightened on the mini-couch, then, still cradling my warm cup, stood up right quick.

I felt a sting on my butt and knew Kayla had pinched me again. Turning back, I gave her a wide-eyed look with a little shrug. She'd be able to read my confusion, because she was hella good at knowing just what I felt. Instead of offering up a little twinkle of sympathy for my embarrassment, she was grinning all wide, which made me wonder if she maybe had somethin' to do with this.

I was straight whupping her ass later, if I found out

she'd set this up. Turning away from my cousin, I followed Darian outside.

The rain was splatting hella hard again, sheets sliding off the overhang of the building, causing a ruckus of noise as they smacked the cement. But it also acted like a curtain, a wall of water blocking a good vision of the parking lot.

We walked in silence, Darian leading the way until we'd cleared the huge plate-glass windows that made up the walls of Starbucks. I knew he was walking far enough so they couldn't see us. My stomach flipped, not sure if I should be excited or nervous.

"What's goin' on?" I asked when he finally stopped walking and turned toward me.

He shrugged, and I could tell he was a little nervous, which helped cool me out. "Just wanted to talk for a minute."

"Just? For *just,* we coulda stayed inside," I replied, pretending to shiver as I snuggled my steaming cup closer to absorb the warmth. Really, I didn't need that, 'cause my body was plenty hot already. But the pretend shiver of cold was a good disguise of my real issue. The tremble of nerves.

He didn't wanna talk to me outside, in the rain, just because. The boy wanted something.

"You're cold?" His hand landed on my upper arm, and tugged me a little closer, then with ease turned us so my back was toward the wall and his body was shielding me from the rain and cold.

He didn't stand close enough to touch, but he was close enough where I could feel the heat of his breath wash across my skin. "Better?"

I glanced up at him and smiled. "Yeah." Then slid my gaze away to watch the plump raindrops. When I tucked my bottom lip between my teeth to keep them from chattering, he made some little noise, so I brought my eyes back to his face and waited for him to tell me what we were really doing out here.

"You were bangin' last night."

I laughed. "And sweats aren't bangin'," I teased, fishing for compliments, I guess, but hell no did I want him telling me I looked good last night but today I look like shit.

"Nah, girl, you top-notch in sweats, too." He looked me up from K-Swiss to outta control curls as he spoke.

"Thanks—" I laughed, then holding the cup with one hand, used the other to hold on to his oversize Creekside hoodie, added "—you're not so bad, either."

He nodded with a confident smile, licking his full lips. "I was wondering, Imani, you have a man?"

Right quick my mind flashed to Maurice and it was undeniable that my body reacted to his image with shooting pulse and heat in my belly in a way that Darian didn't cause. Feelings or not, I was through chasing him.

I shook my head. "Nah."

His smile widened. "So can we hang, just marinate some?"

Can we hang, just marinate? Not entirely sure what he was asking me, I took a sec before I answered. Fa sheezy, though, that can't be how dudes at Creekside ask a girl out. And I wasn't ready for all that anyhow, if that's what he was talking 'bout.

"We can get to know each, Darian. Is that what you want?"

"Yeah, girl. And this." And before I knew what he meant, he was leaning close and his lips touched mine. Softly, at first, he just nipped my bottom lips where I'd had my teeth earlier. Then he kissed me a little fuller, opening his mouth on mine.

Closing my eyes, I tried to absorb the feeling, the smooth sweep of his tongue. He shifted closer, his body keeping me against the wall, but not close enough that we were pressed together, thanks to the latte I was holding.

And then he backed off the kiss just when I was diggin' it, dropping a few quick pecks before he pulled completely away, and turned his head toward Starbucks' door. It didn't take long to see why he'd ended the kiss.

A crowd was startin' to gather at the front of the building, shouts increasing over the rain's noise. As I scanned to see what was going on, my gaze stumbled over dark eyes glaring at me. Maurice's. Even from the distance I was standing, I could see he was mad, by the set of his jaw and hands curled into fists at his side.

It was pretty damn clear that he'd watched the entire kiss, but what did I care? And why should he? I was never his girl. We never did more than talk a few times, and last night he'd made it real obvious that he was cool playin'; but I guess when it comes to me, he was a hater.

"There's a fight," Darian said, stepping away, but taking my hand in his. I tried to pull it away. We weren't like that. I wasn't a bopper, and despite lettin' him kiss me I wasn't ready to be claimed by him.

But his grip was insistent and he pulled me along as he started walking. At least by the time we'd gotten closer I was able to guide him to the other side of the gathering circle, the opposite way from where I'd seen Maurice. I wasn't 'bout to play games with him, and I fo' sho' didn't want him saying something to Darian.

As we shoved closer into the crowd, I could see what was going down. Kayla's friend Leza was getting her ass whupped by Jonathan's girl. Michelle was no joke, straight going savage and dropping fists on point into Leza's face.

Tearing my eyes off the brawl, I glanced around the circle, and caught sight of Jonathan, looking hella smug with his arms folded across his chest as he watched the bootches fight over him.

Wiggling my fingers, I loosed Darian's hold and

pulled my hand free, my gaze roaming away from Jonathan to look for Maurice, realizing that Darian and Maurice both went to Creekside, and if Maurice had real beef, there wouldn't be shit I could do to squash it while they were at school.

And pow—just like it occurred to me that Leza was gettin' thumped on because of me, and Gettin-Hooked.com. Aww, lawdy, I couldn't let this go down. Shoving my shoulder between a couple of yelling people, I dropped my latte to the cement and jumped into the mess, grabbing Michelle's arms and trying to hold her back.

Seeing I was getting involved others started helping, too, taking Leza and dragging her from the ground. Michelle was fighting me hexa hard, and some dude I didn't know helped hold her back.

"Stay away from my man, slut!" she screeched.

"He wanted *me* last night!"

See now, the girl had been gettin' beat down, why the hell didn't she just shut up? Leza's taunt caused Michelle to double her efforts at getting past me. "Bitch! You're a sleaze, give it up, bitch!" Michelle's arm snaked out toward Leza but caught me in the eye.

There were stars for a right quick sec, and I shook my head to clear 'em. Luckily by then the crowd had shifted all the way between them and Leza was being pulled away and Michelle subdued.

A few more minutes and the crowd started to disburse, people realizing the excitement was over so they went back to doing their own thang. Jonathan came up and I figured that was my out. Just as I was moving away my cell buzzed, so I flipped it open and read the text from Kayla letting me know she and Dasia were taking Leza home, and if Darian couldn't do it, they'd be back for me.

Glancing around, I looked for Darian. He'd moved back inside Starbucks now and was talking and laughing with some of his boys. Turning away, I decided I'd rather walk home than ride with him. I didn't want 'im trying to kiss me again. Didn't want 'im trying to make some sorta claim on me I didn't feel.

Missing the warmth of my cup of coffee, I folded my arms across my chest and rubbed my upper arms. It was raining like mad, but not all that cold. Still, I'd be soaked by the time I got home, but right now I really didn't care.

Puffing out a few gulps of air and angling toward home, I didn't hear footsteps over the rain until it was too late.

"Imani, hold up," Maurice said, grabbing my sweatshirt firm enough for me to stop.

I closed my eyes but didn't turn. Just his voice did things to me. Bebopped a rhythm in my blood and made my knees feel weak. I took a slow breath, then turned toward him.

"What?"

"You talkin' to Darian now?"

I narrowed my eyes and glared at him, hella tempted to say "yeah" just so he'd leave me alone. I couldn't stand the feelin' of being mad and hurt mixed with this weird need to step into his arms.

He shook me lightly. "Are you?"

"No." I'd meant to ask why he wanted to know, but "no" was all that came out.

"Why you kissing him then?"

"He kissed me." I was freakin' insane. Why was I justifying my kiss with Darian to him? I'm sure he'd done his thang last night with Brie.

"You just let any dude kiss you, then?"

I pulled my shoulder away, forcing his hand to drop from my arm. Um…no, I didn't get down like that. If he was tryin' to say I was ready to give it up on the easy, I'd straight do him like Michelle did Leza.

Stepping back, I planted my fist on my tilted hip, daring him to say it. My heart was pumping all crazy-like, my stomach trembling. "Fa shizzle, baby boy," I said, making my words drip with sarcasm. "A dude wants to kiss, I let him."

We stood in the roar of the rain, in the heat of anger, in the build of something intense and arousing. The moment lingered, the tension splintering down my spine. His dark gaze was on my face, an eyebrow arched into an odd angle. And then he let out a slow breath, and just like that, the something faded.

His shoulders relaxed. A dimple threatened faintly in a single cheek, like he was fighting a smile. "No you don't," he whispered, stepping forward.

He touched my cheek with his fingertips, then his palm settled fully against my skin as he swooped in and kissed me full on the mouth. Nothing tentative, nothing unsure.

Holding me in place with one hand, he stepped even closer, close enough that I could feel his heat and strength. His lush lips opened, his tongue touching mine. He made a slight sound, like maybe something was hurting. There was something in the sound that made me want to soothe him. Made me want to step closer, so close there was no space left between us.

With my eyes closed, my head light from hardly breathing, I slanted my face and let him kiss me. Really kiss me. Until I didn't think I could stand. All that anger raged into other feelings, emotions I wasn't ready to name.

Then the kiss lightened and slowed, his lips toying with mine, teasing and sucking before he lifted his head, the smile glittering in his eyes.

His mouth was damp now, from our kiss and what had remained of my lip gloss, and I had to fight the desire to reach up and wipe the moisture away. Fight the urge to start laughing.

"No you don't," he repeated. "Not any more."

I shook my head; all that garbage I'd said about not giving a shit what Maurice thought was a frickin' lie. I liked the boy, and after that kiss there was no more denying it. But so what. If he thought he could boss me around, tell me I couldn't kiss other fellas while he did what he pleased, banged whatever chick was available, well then he had another thang coming.

I pushed him hard in the chest, catching him off guard. He stumbled back a few steps. "You don't own me, Maurice. I'll kiss whoever I please." And it didn't matter that he was the only one I wanted touchin' me. He wouldn't know that.

"And you want to be kissing Darian?"

I shrugged, then added a smirk.

"Hold up, Imani, you tellin' me he kissed you like that? He made you feel that? He ain't got it like me, and you know it."

I huffed, jamming my hands on my hips again. I shoulda known; this wasn't 'bout me, but his pride. "What I do know, Maurice, is I'm not your girl. And you are not my daddy. You don't set my rules."

"That's not—"

"Leave me alone. Just leave me alone." I shoved him again, turning away. He tried to grab my sweatshirt again, but I sidestepped. "You actin' like you want somethin' that's not being offered ta ya. Go find Brie."

And when I felt the burn of tears gather behind my eyes, I started running and prayed he wouldn't come after me.

CHAPTER 9

"Imani Lane, to the administration office."

Snap, the bell had just rung and I hadn't even taken my seat in my first-period class when the intercom beeped, then called me up. Amidst the laughter, hoots and *oooohhhsss* from my classmates, I gathered my stuff into my pack and flung it over my shoulder, then aimed for my teacher's desk.

"You gettin' suspended?" some dude called across the room.

"Ooohh, Imani's in trouuuuuble," others teased. "Whatcha do, girl?"

There was no guessing why I was being called to the office. I knew exactly why. And though I hadn't been fighting, my eye told a different story. Dark purple beneath my eye and a swollen upper lid stood as evidence that I'd taken the brunt of Michelle's runaway punch.

I shrugged at the class, trying to look all casual, like being called to the office really didn't bother me. They all knew why I was being called up, too. Shoot, word like this travels fast around the folkies at Howard.

My cell had been blowin' up since Saturday evening and my e-mail box had been crammed full with all these fools wantin' the inside info on what had gone down outside of Starbucks.

My classmates kept laughing until Ms. Sanders told everyone to sit down and get out their journals, then she scribbled her initials onto a hall pass and handed it to me.

As I walked down the hall headed for the admin office, I wondered how much I was supposed to tell Mr. Alton, Howard's principal, about the fight, but I was no narc. I'd try to keep Michelle out of trouble as much as possible, because fa sheezy, the fight didn't take place on school property or during a school event, so I wasn't feelin' why it'd be their business.

A fight off campus was for our parents to deal with. Leza may have been folded, but that didn't have junk to do with school. And, I hadn't even been in it, though deep down I couldn't help this whack feelin' that it was still my fault. My fault because of GettinHooked.com and the fact that Jonathan had used my find-a-prom-date site as a way to play his girl.

I let out a low, slow breath when I reached the office,

sort of surprised that Michelle and Jonathan weren't there already. If the fight was being investigated shouldn't those two be questioned, too? Michelle at the very least since she'd been the one who'd put the whuppin' down.

"In here, Miss Lane," Mr. Alton said, sticking his head out his office door right quick.

I followed him inside, and he shut the door behind me, then indicated I should take a seat. Once I'd sat down he moved around to his side of the desk and slumped in his plump leather chair.

"I'm presuming you know why you're here?"

As if on cue my puffy eye started to throb. Or maybe that was my head.

I nodded. *I knew.*

Mr. Alton shook his head, then turned his attention to some papers and started furiously writing notes on a long yellow pad. My hands were hella sweating as I gripped the cold metal armrests, and my pulse raced as I sat in the hard narrow chair.

The bright overhead flourescent lights were making his beak nose shiny and all the half-healed shaving nicks stand out like crazy.

Biting nervously on my lip, I waited for him to speak, but he didn't. Not a single word, just kept on with his with his pen.

It's not like I needed him to tell me what this was all about, but it would have been hexxa nice to hurry up and get on with it. He might as well talk 'bout the fight. Everyone else was.

But he still didn't. After a little bit, I glanced at the clock and realized I'd been sitting there for nearly a half hour staring at his shiny, beaded-with-sweat forehead.

I cleared my throat, just wanting to get on with it, but he didn't react to my prompt. I felt like shit, a cold setting in after my rain-drenching run home. Though all my peeps had been diggin' me for the haps, I'd ignored the text messages and e-mails, deciding on Sunday to stay in bed and play sick for most of the entire day.

Scratch that, I wasn't playin' at it. Between my aching, stuffy head, swollen eye and stomach that had been touched with the twisting of nerves, sick was closer to the truth than a frickin' stretch.

The only reason I'd come to school this morning was because it was easier checkin' in here than trying to explain to Gram—with my busted-up eye—why I was staying home. Since she stays in her room so much, avoiding her Sunday hadn't been an issue, but had I remained in bed today, she'd have been in to see if I was doing okay.

And I wasn't ready to tell her I'd kissed two fiiine boys in one day, and walked away from them both. It was easier to come to school with my friends, to face Mr. Alton, than to lie in bed all day remembering the way Maurice felt. And the way he'd tasted.

Easier gettin' in trouble—if that's what this was—than lying around dwelling on his accusing words. Or the way both fellas had tried to put some sorta claim on me without either of them asking me to be their girl.

Aww, shit, this was crazy to be sitting here in the principal's replaying Saturday. Again. I was hella trippin' for letting those guys bother me at all. I didn't have time for stupid, and both of them had acted straight stupid. Especially Maurice.

Swallowing the lump in my throat and wiping my damp palms across my thighs, I glanced at the clock again as I blew out a frustrated breath. Another ten minutes and the first-period bell would ring and I'd have missed the entire class for nothing.

"Did you wanna talk to me, Mr. Alton?" I asked, trying not to sound annoyed.

"Actually, Imani, I've been waiting for you. I figured there was something you need to tell me."

What-the-hell-evah! The dude was straight hella crazy if he thought I was going to volunteer to sprinkle. I shook my head, adding a quick shrug.

"No? Nothing?"

"Nope."

He wrote something on his pad, then looked back at me. "I can think of a couple of things."

"Like?"

"Like your eye. You want to tell me how that happened?"

"An accident." That was no lie. Michelle's fist wasn't meant for me.

Mr. Alton glared at me for a sec. My heart pumped and I hoped he didn't notice the way my pulse roared along my neck. Or see how my hands shook just slightly.

"Hmmmph, an accident. I see." He wrote some more, then clicked the mouse on his desk, making his computer screen come out of sleep mode. "What about this, then?" He turned his flat-panel screen my way, and fo' sho', the homepage of GettinHooked was pulled up.

"GettinHooked.com," I mumbled, forcing another shrug and strugglin' to keep my voice all casual. Making a Web site wasn't punishable, so I had no idea why he was bringing it up, other than, of course, how Jonathan met Leza and why Michelle kicked Leza's ass.

"Your creation."

"Yeah, so?" Attitude, too much attitude, I knew. I was tryin' to stay out of the mess, not jump into the hot water.

Knowing what I was going to see, I just glanced at it right quick, but my eye caught something just as he turned the screen back toward him.

My heart squeezed all tight, and I leaned forward, trying to get another glimpse at the screen as my lungs burned for a breath.

There was no way—no way possible—that I saw those numbers right. Yesterday we'd been at around six hundred. The member number showing on Mr. Alton's screen was more than two grand. There had to be some sort of mistake. No way was there more than two thousand student from Howard and Creekside registered for Gettin' Hooked.

"There's nothing wrong with creating a Web site, Imani. I'd like to think our staff has encouraged you to think outside the box in this manner."

Leaning back in my chair, I folded my arms across my chest and bit my bottom lip to keep from laughing. Figures Mr. Alton would try to take some kind of credit for the bomb I'd designed with Kayla.

The first-period bell rang, ending the class. Outside voices rose as students made their way to second period.

Lifting a brow, I curled my lip sarcastically and waited for him to go on.

"But I'm a little concerned about some of the things I've been hearing about this Web site. People are getting hooked up? What's that mean to you, Imani? Sex?"

My face flamed. I hadn't talked about sex with my daddy since he'd given me his version of the birds and the bees, and I sure as hell didn't want to have a talk anywhere near sex with Mr. Alton.

Were folks hooking up, hooking up because of my site? Yeah, I knew some of my friends had been having sex because of it. That didn't mean I was. Though maybe prom night. Maybe with the right guy. Maybe prom night with the right guy. If I found him.

I kept my lip square between my teeth, saying nothing to his comment about sex. When he realized I wasn't spilling, he continued.

"And there's been fights."

And I'd known all along that's what this was all about.

"I don't know anything about either of those, Mr. Alton. My Web site is to help my girls find prom dates that aren't guys we've been hanging with since we were five."

"That's it?"

"Yup."

"And your black eye was an accident?"

"Yup."

"I see." He turned his pale brown gaze away from me and started scribbling on his paper again, the silence getting on my nerves.

"Can I go back to class now?" But what I really wanted to do was find a computer and find out what sort of hype my site had attracted and why the membership profiles was off the heezy.

He lifted his face from his crazed note taking. "Not today, Miss Lane."

"What? I'm being suspended?"

The ass actually smirked at me and I had to grip the metal chair arm to keep from reachin' across his desk and straight-up smacking it off his face.

"No. Your father is picking you up."

I spun around in my chair and looked at the door like he'd be there. He wasn't. A shiver of nervous excitement slithered across my skin. "My dad's coming?"

"Yes. You can wait for him in the lobby. I'm finished talking to you."

Oh, he was through. Ha, he had no idea how whack this was. I didn't need to be explaining my site to him. He should deal with school shit, and that's it.

Getting to my feet, my knees trembled a little, but I ignored it and grabbed my backpack off the floor. As I headed toward the office door, I said, "Pixx," and flashed him a peace sign.

When I reached the admin office lobby I plopped back down on a chair to wait for my dad, a little freaked about why he was coming and afraid it meant something bad. I didn't even know he'd landed, and thought he wouldn't be here until Wednesday.

Closing my eyes to ward off a rush of tired and frustrated tears, I leaned my head back, feeling worse every second. Wrapping my arms around my middle, I had to wonder if the chills I'd been having hadn't been annoyance, but really fever.

After a quick sec, I took a deep breath and pulled my cell out of my pocket, then thumbed in a message for Kayla, Pop n twn. 2K GH mem, to let her know I wouldn't be around later and that something was blowin' up with our site.

Just as I hit Send, my dad walked in and I went into his arms.

CHAPTER 10

"I didn't know you were coming in today, Daddy," I said, snuggling into his embrace, not givin' a damn that we were standing in the admin office. Only seeing him a few days a month wasn't enough. But I knew he was gone all the time because he was doing his best for me.

His arms were tight around me, his chest strong and lean. The warm scent of Polo cologne that clung to his clothes was bringing tears to me eyes, reminding me of when I was younger and he'd cradle me close. When his flights had been domestic, rather than international, and he spent more time at home.

"My flight schedules were rearranged."

"What are you doing here?"

He chuckled, the rumble against my cheek familiar and comforting. "I live in this area, in case you didn't know," he said teasingly, one large hand stroking across my hair.

"I mean at school. You came home to me being in

trouble." Snap, I hadn't meant to say that. Mr. Alton was straight trippin' and I hadn't done anything wrong.

My dad put his hands around my shoulders and backed me out of his embrace. "Trouble, Imani?" His gaze landed on my black eye, then his dark eyes narrowed. "What's going on, girl? Talk to me."

"It was an accident. Really," I added when he continued to look at me all skeptical like.

He nodded, but still looked pensive. After a quick sec, he stroked a gentle thumb over my bruised cheekbone. "You win?"

"I wasn't fighting."

With another nod he gave me an odd look, then smiled as he hugged me again, planting a kiss on my temple. "Let me check you out and we'll get out of here." He took my pack. "You can tell me about your trouble in the car."

About ten minutes later we'd escaped the office, made our way through the pouring rain and finally took refuge in his hella clean black Lexus, and I was free of school for the rest of the day. That helped ease my whacked-out, frazzled nerves, but I was still feeling the onset of a cold and the lingering festering of a heart that been used the wrong way.

Cuddling up in the leather seat, I leaned my forehead against the cool glass as my daddy drove. Fat raindrops snaked down the outside window, the clouds thick and darkening around us.

With the soft voice of Usher, my baby-boy, seeping from the speakers thanks to XM Radio, I felt my lids droop and the restless last couple of nights start to ease from my bones. From my tired and sick body.

"Daddy," I said sleepily, "how come you haven't mentioned my trouble?"

He relaxed in his seat, his left elbow on the window frame, his long fingers managing the wheel, his other hand casually tossed over the gearshift. He grinned, then winked. "Because I didn't know about it. You told on yourself, baby."

What the— "How'd you know I was in the office? How'd Mr. Alton know you were coming?"

"I called. Asked them to call you to the office. Thought you could play hooky for the day, spend a little time with me. I'm only home for two days."

He took my hand. "Now don't look so sad, Imani, you know I'd stay longer if I could."

"I know." My words were whispered, but hard to push out they were so lodged in my dry throat. I did know. His schedule was hard on him, too.

Pulling slowly into the breakfast line at McD's, my dad clamped down his foot on the brake and angled more fully toward me. "Why don't you tell me about your eye? Who'd you fight? I'm guessing that's the trouble you were talking about."

I laughed. Fo' sho', parents thought they knew everything. "Not really."

"Oh?"

"I wasn't fighting."

"That's good. So what happened then?"

I sighed, then decided to clue him in on most of what was going down. I'd leave off the double kiss afternoon. No need having my daddy freakin' about the boy situation. No need for my dad's usual threats against any fellas interested in messin' with me.

"Actually, it's about a Web site."

"Go on." He pulled the car up one, bringing us a little closer to the menu board.

"Right. You won't freak, will you?"

My daddy laughed, his hand tightening around mine, it wasn't painful, but reassuring. "I'm cool, baby, but you'd best start talking."

"Kayla and I set up a Web site, like a locals-only MySpace." I watched his face, and lowered my voice. "To get prom dates."

He'd been looking straight ahead and tapping his fingers in rhythm with the song, but as soon as the word *date* slipped past my lips his dark eyes and all his attention were focused on me.

"Prom dates?"

A little anxious giggle bubbled up. "Yeah, Daddy, you know that I've gone to school with the same guys forevah! Prom's supposed to be special, but the fellas at Howard are tapped, played out and tired."

"So how's your cousin figure in?"

"She feels the same way about her friends at Creekside, so our site is set up to kinda...um...er, trade."

"Trade?"

"Fa shizzle. My girls can meet fellas from Creekside. Kayla's peeps can meet fellas from Howard. It's perfect. We all live close. We all needed dates."

We pulled up another spot, easing closer to ordering, the thought causing my stomach to grumble in hunger. With his foot back on the brake, he glanced at me again.

"Look at you, Imani. You're beautiful. I hardly think you'll have any trouble finding a guy to escort you to prom." He chuckled, then shook his head in sympathy. "Poor boy."

I laughed with him. "What's that supposed to mean?" I shrugged and held out my hands, palm up, to my sides.

"Just that you're more than beautiful. You're smart. And special. Some poor fella is going to be a fool for you sometime soon, baby."

"You're my daddy. You're supposed to think I'm pretty and special," I replied, grinning for the first time all morning.

"Nah, it's more than that, Imani. You're like your momma, she was so pretty and sweet."

I held my breath, shock trembling though my system. *Go on, oh, God, go on,* my heart begged, at the same time tears burned behind my eyes. My hands shook, so I folded them in my lap, and kept my gaze trained out the window, just as I had been.

My momma was a non-topic, and I can't remember the last time, if ever, my daddy had spoken about her calmly. And the few memories I do have, he'd been filled with anger and bitter.

I swallowed right quick, then licked my lips, trying to find a little moisture. *...like your momma, she was so pretty and sweet...* Those words had been said softly and filled with such tenderness.

It felt good, hella good to hear him talk about her like she'd actually been a part of his life rather than a big blank. But the light feeling was quickly overshadowed by something else.

Fear.

Had something happened to her? I'm not sure why it mattered, since it'd been such a long time since she'd been in my life anyway, but a gnawing burn started in my gut and wouldn't quit.

The pieces seemed to fit. First my auntie's phone call, and this gut feeling that she'd been talkin' about me. Then there'd been the pictures that Gram had hidden under her book. The envelope. And now my daddy talking 'bout her like she'd passed.

I swallowed again, choking down the lump of raw pain. "Daddy?" My voice cracked, and his gaze swiveled to my face.

"Hmm?"

"Is my momma dead?"

His shoulders seemed to deflate, a whistled breath rushing past his lips. He remained casually reclined in his leather seat, but I could see the tension in the way his knuckles gripped the wheel. In the way his jaw clenched. I could feel the tension tapdancing along my spine.

Finally, after a dragged-out moment, he said, "I don't know, baby." He shrugged. "I don't know where she's at. I quit keeping track when you were about ten."

And lawdy, that hurt nearly as bad, something sharp and hot pierced my chest and left me feeling empty and sad. Being dead woulda been a hexa good excuse for droppin' out my life and staying gone. Just being gone meant she really didn't have any interest in being my momma at all.

And I knew that already. I knew she walked out on me. *Her loss,* I silently repeated, the same reassurance I always brushed up on.

"Wh—" I had to break off to get the tears out of my throat and to wipe the trails of liquid from my cheeks. "Why'd she leave?"

Seventeen and I'd never once asked him direct.

His hand gripped mine, firm but expressing emotion. "Imani, baby, I wish I could give you the answers you deserve. I loved the girl." He shook his head. "I loved the girl, and if she wanted to leave me, I'd have been hurt but would've dealt with it. She had no right to leave you."

I gulped. "And that's why you've never forgiven her?"

"She hasn't asked for forgiveness. That requires she repent. If she isn't dead, baby, then her years and years of silence, of staying away, tells me she's not sorry. I can't forgive that."

My lips were quivering so bad I had to tuck my lower one between my teeth, and there was no stopping the silent tears as they poured over my lashes.

"Hey, pretty girl," my daddy said, putting a big palm across my cheek and swiping away the silver trails. "I love you very much. Your momma may not want you, but, baby, I do. I couldn't be prouder of my girl."

His thumb smoothed across my plump and bruised eye, causing me to suck my teeth and wince.

"Even with your busted-up eye." He laughed, then, looking forward, he eased his foot off the brake and pulled up to the menu. With a touch of his fingertip, his window went down all smooth. He smiled at me and I knew in that smile that his words were true. "You ready to order?"

I forced a smile. "Yeah. And we should take something to Gram, too."

And then we went on to order some food and while my daddy paid and we waited for it to be prepped and bagged, I eased back into my seat and watched the rain fall noisily across the glass, then slide downward, just like my eyelids.

As I drifted in the haze of half consciousness and half sleep, I realized that today could be one of those lazy days where we lounge around, watch movies, eat popcorn and just spend the day as a family, safe from the weather. Safe from the world.

And today I could ditch school—with my daddy's help—and I could take cold medication, and forget about classes, homework, friends. Forget about my poppin' off outta control Web site. Forget about boys and prom dates.

Forget about kisses, and dark, dark eyes that stroked my soul and made me want something.

Today was a day of forgetting and getting onward. Exactly what I needed. My daddy and home and sleep.

CHAPTER 11

MY daddy had dropped me off back at school Wednesday morning on his way to the airport again. I hadn't been ready to see him go, but after being home all day Monday and Tuesday, sleeping and getting the tender care of Gram's chicken and dumplings, I'd been ready to see my peeps again.

In those two days of being home, I'd kept my cell off and had gotten online once, but then it had only been to check GettinHooked's numbers. Tuesday afternoon they'd been 3,204.

And I found a problem. A hella huge frickin' problem. All of 'em weren't just from Howard and Creekside. Like stuff always goes down, someone had told someone else who then flapped their lips, and word had spread. GettinHooked was off the chain, and had spread across the entire area.

GettinHooked was bumping, straight blowing up.

There were so many people now that they were just making dates on their own, hooking up, when they exchanged e-mails and messages. I wasn't involved in the planning anymore, and I fo' sho' doubted Kayla was, either.

Feel apprehensive about all the area schools getting their sticky fingers into our find-a-prom-date idea, I'd sent Kayla a message, letting her know why I was home, and asking her what we should do about the jumping, pumping numbers.

She'd instantly e-mailed back, Nothing. It's hot. And I met a guy. I tried to ask her about 'im, but she must've gotten offline right after hitting Send 'cause she'd quit replying to my messages. And I'd gone back to my spot on the couch anyway, to spend the time with my daddy. Even Gram joined us, deciding to venture from her room.

And I'd hardly checked the site or talked to Kayla after that, because returning to school on Wednesday had been hexa jacked, filled with makeup work and trying to catch up on missed exams, the messed-up thang about not being at school. And there'd been a lot to catch up on, too, since we were steppin' from school for the next ten days for spring break, so tests and junk were on double uptake.

And the fact that we were at spring break already freaked me the hell out. Snap, less than three weeks after that was prom. Three weeks after chillin' and marinatin' while off school, and I was still no closer to having the perfect prom date than I was when I'd thought up this mess in the first place.

Trying not to think about it, I spent the week studying, my head in a book rather than on my dateless prom, and the fellas I had to choose from. At least my girls had been hooking up like mad, finding dudes to go along with their pre-picked dresses. And from Kayla's less frequent messages, she had a boy spittin' at her, too.

Shortened to a three-day school week, it still dragged on hella long, and I'd gotten to the point that I was avoiding the scrubs and beezies at Howard who wanted inside tracks on hook-ups because this whole thang had gotten out of hand.

By Friday I was more than ready to blow school and spend some time postin' with Kayla. I'd already told Gram I was headed to my cousin's right after school, so as soon as the bell rang after American Government, I headed toward her house rather than home.

The walk wasn't far, and I spent most of it scrolling through text messages I hadn't answered all week. Nothing really important, just "what ups" and "where you beens," except there were a few messages from Darian, too, that I'd done a pretty good job ignoring.

It's not that I didn't dig the boy. He was fine, and seemed into me, but somethin' kept me from wanting to get to know him better.

Maurice.

And the fact that I hadn't been able to get him from my mind since he kissed me bugged and nagged at me. Not even while sick and sleepy had the memory of his mouth on mine been far off, and a couple times I'd been tempted to head back to the computer to check out his profile. Again. But I hadn't.

I just felt so hella confused, because despite pushing 'im away and refusing to be bossed 'round by him, if there was a fella I wanted to spend time with, it was Maurice. Not Darian.

It was all gravity, though; hell no was I wasting time trippin'. I wasn't a bopper, or a girl that'd let a dude get over. If either of them wanted to get at me, they'd have to step correct.

Slushing my sneakers along the sidewalk, my pace slow, the cool air on my cheeks froze up the increasing heat on my cheeks as I drew closer to Kayla's. And Maurice's. I had this weird crazy need to stay away from the boy, to not look into his hella fine face, or into dark eyes that made my stomach feel warm and my heart rate pick up speed.

Thinking of him, wondering about him did funny thangs to me. Made my pulse race. Made me want to smile. And cry. And all that bent out of shape emotion was running amok on how I was dealin' with shit. Seeing him made it worse.

And even though I'd peeped him a couple times throughout the week, once while out with my dad and another after school Thursday, I'd straight dodged him, doing everything I could to avoid him.

Pausing at the end of the cul-de-sac, I could only hope he wasn't outside today since it had at last quit raining. I took a few steadying breaths, then made my way around the corner so I could peep into the court, hoping the street was silent and empty.

Breathing a sigh of relief when I didn't see Maurice, or anyone else, I lingered, hesitant, but also knowing he could drive around the corner any sec in his hella clean black Altima and see me standing here like a damn fool.

Sliding my pack from my shoulders, I reached into the front pocket and shuffled through for my iPod, then popped the tiny buds into my ears, found a bangin' song and smashed my thumb gently to make it play. At least with music ring-a-dingin' I'd be able to pretend to not notice Maurice if he did come out before I made it inside Kayla's. Or I'd be able to make ignoring him seem reasonable.

Scoffing at myself, I flung my backpack on again, and headed down the court, my pace quicker now, and careful to keep my face forward and my gaze schooled, not trailin' off toward his place. And before I knew it, I was heading around to the side gate of my cousin's house to go in through the kitchen, and without having to deal with seeing Maurice.

The slider was open, as usual, so I let myself in. Besides Kayla, the house was wiped out, my auntie and uncle gone on a ten-day Alaskan cruise and Brandon staying with our unshared gramma, his dad's side, for spring vacation.

Music echoed down the hallway from upstairs, so I jogged up to Kayla's room, tapping my knuckles against the door as I let myself in.

"What's crack-a-lackin'?" I said, dropping into the beanbag chair, tossing my backpack aside as I tucked my headphones back into the front pocket and put my iPod away.

She grinned at me, looking up with blue eyes so bright I knew something was up with her.

"Hey, girl." She whispered the greeting, but I could tell she was listening to someone else. Sitting on the floor, the phone propped between her ear and shoulder, her legs spread out into a wide V, pictures scattered on the carpet between, she was wiggling her bare toes to the rhythm of Diddy.

After a sec, she picked up a picture and handed it to me, her lips forming the word "fine" but not a sound seeping out. I laughed as I accepted the picture that had been printed off the computer, angling it so I could check it out.

Oh, yeah, the boy was a hottie, all right. A light-skinned brotha, with cornrows braided into his hair and hazel eyes that twinkled like he was 'bout to get over.

Kayla giggled at something said on the other end of the phone, her laughter drawing my attention right quick from the pic she'd handed me.

"Who dat is?" I asked.

She wiggled her pale brows, then lifted a second picture from the floor and handed it my way. The same fella, just a different pose. A different day, judging by the hair, now in a tight fade.

"He's *cute*."

"Yup." She handed me a few more pictures to check out, then turned her attention back to the caller. "Hey, lemme call you back, 'kay? My cousin's here."

She was quiet for a quick min, only Diddy's voice interrupting the silence, and while Kayla listened to what some boy was spittin' at her, my gaze slowly drifted to the window, and my mind to Maurice.

Was he at home? Was he chillin' with Brie? Had they hooked up? And why had he been so demanding, why had he kissed me? Was there something more than his busted-up pride at steak?

"Oh, my God, I like that boy," Kayla said, her tone light with joy, drawing my attention back to her.

"He's a boy? He looks older. Where he from?"

"Chicago, but he's in Arizona now." She reached forward, blond strands falling in her face as she gently touched my cheek. "Your eye doesn't look too bad."

I knew what the girl was about, trying to change the subject, thinking I might miss the mention of her diggin' a dude from another state. "Much better than it was," I replied, smoothing my fingertips across skin that had been so tender a few days back.

"That was crazy. Did Michelle get suspended?"

"Nah, but can you believe how messed up it is that Mr. Alton tried to make me take some blame?" And in a way I knew he was been right: some of the responsibility did lie on my Web site.

"Messed up, Imani. I'm glad you didn't get in trouble though."

"Me, too." I lifted a different photo, slanting it foward, wanting to get back to this guy and the mention of Arizona. "What's his name?"

"James Drew, isn't he so frickin' hot."

"How you meet him?"

Her cheeks went from pale peaches to strawberry in the thump of a heartbeat. "Gettin' Hooked."

"Gettin' Hooked! Kayla, you gotta be kiddin' me." Panic started speeding through my blood as I pushed off the beanbag and went to her desk to flick on her computer.

I knew our profiles numbers were insane now, but I'd

assumed they were all semilocal high schools wanting on board. But if Kayla was talking to someone out of state, then our Web site had to be all over the freakin' place now.

"He's a Sun Devil. A freshman at Arizona State."

The computer was taking a sec to come out of sleep mode. "In college, Kayla, dayum."

My hands were trembling as I scrolled the mouse through some of the new profile pages, the browser laggin' probably because of how huge the site had become.

"He's just nineteen, though," she mumbled, her tone just sharp enough to sound a little defensive.

"Is this the guy you were telling me about?"

"Nope." She moved in behind me, the pictures that had been on the floor gathered into a stack in her hand. Kneeling right behind me, she reached over and took control of the mouse. "This is him." She clicked on a profile.

"Chris Lewis," I said, not needing to read his name. He went to Howard and I'd known him since we were eleven. "He's nice. What happened to diggin' him? You were hella hyped on him all week."

"Nah, just for a few days, not all week. And besides, that was before I peeped out this boy." She dropped the photos onto the desk.

"So you're just blowing Chris off?"

Kayla shrugged, but I could see the guilt in her blue eyes and by the way she kept looking away, unable to meet my gaze. I knew this girl and there wasn't much she could hide from me.

"We were supposed to go out tonight, but I told him my parents said another time."

"Your parents aren't even home."

She laughed. "I know."

My mouth plopped open as I stared at my cousin, having a hard time figuring out what was going on with her. She'd grabbed up all her hair and was busy twisting it into a braid.

"Darian said you're not callin' him back."

She brought up Darian to change the subject again. And just like she'd closed down, I wasn't in the mood to share, either. A first for us. It was hecka weird. I forced a smile and shrugged. "I will."

Pushing away from the computer, I got to my feet, then took her hand and yanked her up. "Come on, I'm starved. Let's find grub and put on a movie or something. Then we can decide what's up for later tonight."

"Okay, Imani, nice one." She laughed as she shut off Diddy and followed me out of her tie-dyed room and down the hall. "Don't talk. I see how it is, girlfriend."

"Fa shizzle, Kayla. I'm just hungry."

"Riiiight." She made a clicking sound with her lips, and when I turned and glanced at her she was rolling her eyes at me. "But you should know—" She giggled. "Darian got it bad for you. What's going on with you two? I was kinda feelin' you and Maurice hooking up."

I paused, turning to look at her. "Why you think that?"

"He asks about you, is all." She tugged on my hand, swinging our arms like we did when we were little. "Besides, he looks at you different. I don't know how to describe it, just different. Like warm or somethin' crazy. And he did put his number in your phone."

"He didn't ask me to call him though."

"He needed to ask? I'd have thought the digits programmed in woulda been a clue and a half."

"Guess I'm clueless then."

"Look atcha, a playa playa with two hella fiiine boys on the hook. Which one you want, Maurice or Darian?"

I laughed, but that nagging guilt started coiling up in my gut. I didn't want Darian liking me like that because I was fo' sho' not going to return it. "Whatevah. Feed me."

And with that our conversation fell away from boys for a bit, chatting instead about what we were gonna eat and what flick we were gonna put on. And it felt cool just hanging out, just the two of us.

CHAPTER 12

"**what's** wrong with you, Kayla? I've been sug-gesting shit to do tonight for the last hour and you're doing nothing but throwing tude. What the hell?"

"Whatevah, Imani. Maybe I'm just not in the mood to party."

I took a deep breath and held it for a sec, trying to let some of my tension go, but it was wound so tight that it making me see red and feel nothing but annoyed. "Of course not, Kay, you want to stay here and talk to some guy who lives states away. Sure thang, girlie, makes sense to me."

Kayla and I had munched down on Ritz crackers and sliced salami, then brushed off all the crumbs and lounged on the sofa in front of her big screen and watched *Step Up* for the hundredth time, admiring the white boy with dance moves. Besides, Mario was in it and it made me want to get up and shake-shake my groove thing.

Usually we laughed and talked and giggled over the movie since we'd seen it so many times, but today we sat in silence, Kayla totally distracted by a flood of text messages blowin' up her cell.

"Nothing's wrong with wanting to stay home and talk to a dude I like. Maybe you should try it."

I shoved a chenille throw to the side and stood up, turning toward her with my hands on my hips. "Maybe I should try it? Hmmm, lemme think about it. Talk to a fella while dissin' my cousin or realize where my blood is."

"Whatevah, Imani. I'm not forgettin' you're my blood, but I like this guy. I want to get to know him."

"And how you gonna do that? With texts? He doesn't even live around here."

Kayla closed her cell for the first time all night. "So what?"

"So what!" I was losing my temper now, damn irked that she didn't get it. "You met some guy on Gettin-Hooked.com who lives in Arizona. Who's in college. This was supposed to be about Howard and Creekside. Only. A local MySpace, remember?"

Kayla reached for the remote and turned the TV hella loud, then sank back into the cushions and opened her phone when it beeped, proceeding to ignore me.

Aww, hell no. "That's f'd up, Kayla!" I shouted to

be heard over the bass bumping from the surround sound speakers.

"You're not always right, you know!"

"But I'm right about this. GettinHooked needs to be shut down. My friends are fighting, peeps are using it to cheat. This whole frickin' thing was so we could get hooked up with prom dates. How the fuck you gonna go to prom with James Drew, Chicago transplant to 'Zona!"

"Maybe I'm not as obsessed as you. Maybe I don't give a shit about prom."

I stood there gaping at her, my hands balled into fists, my body trembling, a funky haze of anger straight up tainting the entire room. I took a deep breath, squeezing my lids closed as I tried to put myself in check.

Letting out the breath slowly, I lowered my voice and looked at Kayla as she fiddled a message into text. "We have to shut down the site."

"Hell no."

"We *haaaave* to. It's not right. It's not how I wanted it."

"No, Imani, peeps love the site. They'd be hella mad at us."

"They're gonna be mad at us anyway, when they find out they're gettin' creeped on. They can go back to MySpace. That was hexa fun, everyone loved it before this site anyway."

"Not happenin', girl, I think it's hot."

I clenched my jaw, and felt my nostrils flaring. I was straight up on the verge of a two-year-old tantrum, stomping feet and all. I gulped, trying unsuccessfully not to scream. "Kayla, we have to. This isn't the way it was supposed to be."

"It's better."

She shook her head, the smooth strands of her hair coming free from the quick braid she'd twisted up earlier. "No, it's not outta control. It's straight off the heezy."

"We gotta shut it down. Somethin' bad's gonna happen." I touched my stomach, trying to show her the knots of dread growing there. "I just feel it." My hands were shaking, the combination of tension and arguing with my cousin hella bothering me.

"You're trippin'."

And maybe I was. Maybe she was right about that. Things just felt like they were mounting up and then pressing down on me. Everything, from being sick, to missing my daddy, to wondering what my Gram was hiding, to feeling so torn between Maurice and Darian and trying to sort out how I felt about each of them.

Grabbing the remote, I lowered the volume and brought my voice down, too. "Then we gotta at least find a way to keep it local, like it was meant to be."

"Hell no. We already got folks from all over. What we supposed to do, kick 'em off?"

"Yeah. They weren't supposed to be there. We were supposed to use student IDs to log in."

"Everyone has student IDs, Imani."

And that was exactly where we'd gone wrong. We hadn't thought of the possibility that anyone else from any other area would give a damn about out little hook-up site. We'd trade, like I told my dad. Girls would find guys and guys would find girls at each other's schools. This was about prom, nothing else. Nothing more.

If it wasn't meant for locals only, what would be the point? We'd have left it as MySpace if we wanted worldwide. We wanted datable.

"How's a college dude have a high school student ID?"

She smirked. "Oh, so that's what this is all about. You're jealous? I didn't think I'd get that from you."

"Kayla, I am not jealous!"

"That's right, you playin' two dudes."

Oh, lawdy, I almost gave my cousin an eye to match my bruised and swollen one. I swallowed, bile rising up from my gut, my pulse roaring in my ears. She didn't mean it. I knew deep in my gut she didn't, that her words were dripping with anger, but they cut just the same.

Still, there was no defending, no comeback to her words. I had to bounce, to get the hell out of there before I said somethin' I'd regret. Before she flapped her lips some more and this argument turned into a fight.

"All righty, then. I'm outie." And I didn't look back as I retrieved my backpack then split, retracing my usual steps out the kitchen slider. She didn't once try to stop me.

It was dark now, but I didn't give a shit. The cool air felt good on my face, the dampness of the night helped ease the dry ache in my throat and the moisture in the air helped disguise the mist lingering in my eyes.

I can't remember the last time Kayla and I had argued, but it'd been so long ago in all likelihood it'd been about some little-girl junk like who was playing with which Barbie.

Rounding the house, I didn't even bother slowing when I noticed the garage door at Maurice's was open and that I could hear his voice laughing with his boys from just inside, see their shadows and silhouettes.

Pulling up my hoodie, I tucked my hair inside and kept walking hexa fast down the street, fighting hard against the need to scroll through my cell phone, find the number Maurice had put in and dial it. See if he could drive me home. There were plenty of times where I loved this walk, enjoyed the time to cool out and be alone with my thoughts. Tonight wasn't one of 'em.

The darkness poured over me, the low lingering clouds wrapping around me just like my loneliness.

A few houses farther, I slowed to listen to the chirping crickets silly enough to brave the cold, to a car stroll across the pavement someplace out of view, to the low *thump-a-thump* of bass bumping from somebody's ride, the low boom filling the night.

I stood in the shadows, out of reach of the milky light of the streetlamp, and watched his house, my gaze lazily drifting back and forth between his place and my cousin's.

Time hung suspended until my body lost some of the anger, and my heart raced, picking up speed for a different reason, I knew it was time to bounce. Not only was Maurice with the fellas tonight, but I just didn't have it in me to deal with him.

Not with Kayla losin' her mind the way she was. Fa sheezy, when my uncle came back from their cruise I was straight-up asking him for his help to get this outta control site mess untangled. My site idea was a good one, and I was straight-up proud of its success, but maybe because it'd been my idea in the first place I also felt partially responsible for some of the chaos.

And it was just gonna get uglier, *funkier,* I was sure of it.

With my shoulders saggin', I quit glancing at Kayla's and tore my gaze from where Maurice was postin', then moved toward home. Friday night, the start of vacation, and the night was whack.

Though I wasn't feeling the full effects of my cold anymore, I wasn't all the way recovered; the throbbin' at my temples was increasing, along with the pressure holding up on my sinuses.

The mile didn't take long, and after twenty minutes of steady walkin' I was easing my key from my backpack and quietly letting myself in. The condo was dim, lit up only by the pale gray moonlight that worked its way through the clouds and by the changing lights of the TV that shifted across the carpet from beneath my gram's bedroom door.

Dropping my things on the love seat, I moved to her room, and despite it being after ten, I knocked gently on the door, then peeked my head inside. "Gram, just wanted to let you know I'm home."

She was in bed mostly asleep, but she lifted a hand and mumbled something. I always let her know when I come in, no matter what time. I didn't want her to hear the door and be frightened, especially on a night I'd planned on being gone at Kayla's.

That done, I found my way down the short hallway to my room, kicked off my sneakers and walked in my socks to my bed. No caring about my jeans or my school-pride hoodie, I climbed under the comforter and lay curled on my side.

And no matter how I tried not to, I cried. Turning my face into the pillow, I inhaled, then the tears started coming. A silent pathetic cry, where the sobs shook my entire body and the slightest sound I made was captured in the cotton of my bedding.

Things were so messed up, and I felt so helpless, with no one to turn to. This is the sorta thing most girls would turn to their mommas about, but I didn't have one. My auntie had been there for a lot, but she wasn't here now. Gram was in the next room, but I didn't feel right about burdening her with my junk, and Daddy was flying someplace, with no way to reach him.

So the tears came, leaving my pillow damp and my cheeks slick, and my soul feelin' hella empty. I cried it out. About fighting with Kayla, about my missin' momma, about Maurice first kissing me, then getting bossy, and about Darian, who seemed to like me, but I couldn't find it in me to like 'im back.

Even when the tears had dried and the sobs decreased into sniffles and whimpers, even when my eyes burned and drooped closed and my head ached nearly as bad as my heart did, even when the clock ticked way past midnight, sleep didn't come. Sleep hovered outta reach, leaving me instead tired but totally restless.

Things had gotten jacked and tomorrow I was determined to start settin' things back to rights.

CHAPTER 13

I'M not sure when sleep finally won out, but I do know it was well after the deep hues of nighttime started to brighten to purple as the sun kissed the distant horizon. And when it finally came, it was the sort of hella hard sleep where I hardly moved and time passes hexa quickly.

Stretching onto my back, trying to untwist the material around me, I wished I'd taken the time the night before to get out of my jeans and sweatshirt.

Rubbing the heel of my palm across my eyes, taking special care of the lingering bruise, I wiped the sleep from my eyes and glanced wearily toward my clock. The green digital display read 9:42 and sun, bright-ass sun, had finally been able to get in through all the clouds and filled my room with golden shimmering beams.

It wasn't much, but at least a couple of hours were

better than no sleep at all. Suppressing a yawn with the back of one hand, I reached my other into my pocket and yanked out my cell, flipping it open right quick to call Kayla. Fo' sho', we needed to talk. Bad.

Her phone rang four times, then into her voice-mail. I hung up and dialed again, but the same crazy thang happened: her voice came on tellin' me to fill up her inbox and she'd get back at me.

"Kayla," I said, then paused to gather my thoughts right quick before going on. "Kay, we need to talk. Holla back."

Figuring she could still be sleeping, I decided to shower and get something to eat while I waited on my girl. We'd be cool again as soon as we talked, worked shit out, I decided, feeling hella better about things this morning since I'd purged up so much emotion last night.

Still laggin' like crazy, I took my time showering, lingering in the warm spray, lathering in the sweet-scented soap, washing my hair and then letting it sit with conditioner for a bit.

By the time I was out and dressed a couple hours had passed and my stomach was frickin' growling, only having had cheese and crackers for dinner the night before.

I tried Kayla again, but ended up in her voice-mail just like before. I left another message, then went to ask

Gram if she wanted something to eat. She said no, but I decided I'd get her some of whatever I was gonna fix myself anyway.

Takin' some pastrami out of the fridge, I placed a heaping pile in the micro. I crossed my feet and leaned my elbows back onto the smooth black granite countertop to wait, and started wondering if Kayla was sleeping hella late or if she was gonna straight up ignore me.

I knew she was mad, I knew she was hexa hyped about this James guy and I had to admit he was hot. The girlie had good taste in dudes, but even as fine as he was, it didn't make up for the fact that he lived too far away to take her to prom. And whether she wanted to admit it or not, that was the point.

Jealousy…she'd accused me of it, so while I waited for the final minute of heat time to unwind, I couldn't help wondering if just the slightest little piece of her accusation might be true. Not that I wanted the boy she did, but rather, maybe she'd been sayin' I was envious of the fact that she liked someone who liked her back? No more questioning? No insecurity?

Beep, beep, beep. The time had gotten away from me, so the shrill alarm startled me. My heart jumped into my throat, my hands shook all crazy like for a sec. Taking a deep breath, I tried to chill, then slowly reached for the plate of hot food and filled two rolls with the steaming meat.

After filling up a couple of glasses of Gram's sweet tea, I took her a plate, then took mine to my room to try e-mailing Kayla instead of calling.

I checked GettinHooked again, too, and saw the numbers had risen, but at least not as freakin' much as before. Scrolling though the profiles, I peeped fellas from all across the country, a few as far away as Alaska, all hyped on getting with a skeeza.

Waiting for Kayla to reply, I moved through the pages until I landed on James Drew, and found all the pics that Kayla had printed scattered across his profile. I read over his profile, from the info on his high school back in Chicago to where he was talkin' about his college major.

He was cute, and if his profile was legit, he didn't seem like that bad a guy for Kayla. Except he lived in another state, too far to be her man, and fa sheezy too far to be the right date on prom night.

I was sitting there reading over James's info and like and dislike lists when I spotted a mention of spring break. Looking closer at the dates Arizona State were out, I realized they had pretty frickin' close to ours.

And this hella funny feeling came over me. "You wouldn't," I mumbled, dialing Kayla's cell again, but getting nothing. "Please tell me you wouldn't.

Following through with my gut feeling, I hit the contact page on James's page and sent him an e-mail right quick, and hoped like mad he'd get back to me soon.

It was nearly five in the afternoon, the sunshine already starting to fade, clouds silently rolling back in and I still hadn't heard a peep from my cousin. And still, after exploding her box until it couldn't hang with any more of my messages, she hadn't responded.

And neither had James.

But panic had started.

Sliding my feet into some Jordans and grabbing my house key and cell, I stepped out of my condo, moved across the street, then straight started to run, dusk hella heavy now, the shadows lengthening as the sun caressed the skyline.

I was breathing hecka hard by the time I rounded the corner into her cul-de-sac about a mile away from my place. The streetlights had just clicked on, but inside Kayla's was completely dark. Jogging around the side, I moved the slider and found it locked tight.

I banged a couple of times, yanking hard on the handle and knowing damn well even if I'd gotten it open I didn't know the code to the home alarm.

I gripped my phone, my hands shaking so bad I could hardly hit the button for speed dial. The "System full" message played, telling me she still hadn't checked messages.

I ran around front, smacking the door, ringing the doorbell over and over. "Kayla! Kayla!" I hit the door again, kicking the frame as fear and frustration gathered hot liquid in my eyes.

"Kay, please! Open the door." I knew she wasn't in there. Using my hoodie sleeve, I wiped tears from my cheeks, then turned and sat down on the cement front steps, my knees shaking too bad to keep me upright.

"Shit," I hissed, scrolling through the numbers in my phone, looking for their grandma's where Brandon was stayin', but it didn't take long to realize I didn't have it anymore.

"Shit, Kayla, please tell me you didn't." Desperation made me dial her line again, then hit Redial as soon as her box came up. I bit down on my bottom lip to keep it from quivering, to keep the sobs from cuttin' loose.

The light was fading quick, and I sat there with no idea what to do. My heart was racing, my body trembling as I struggled to reason out why she'd have bailed, wondering how long she'd been planning this.

Unsure of what else to do, I decided to tell Gram, because I had no idea what I could do to get Kayla back—and I knew fo' sho' she'd taken off to 'Zona to meet that dude.

And the scariest part of all: who knew if James was really who he said he was? He could be a grown-ass man with a thing for underage girls, fa shizzle, I'd heard the same sort of story enough times on the news.

Now Kayla could fall victim, lured to another state

all thanks to my site, and if I'd had any itty-bitty doubt before, it was gone now. That whacked-out site had to get shut down. It was too freakin' damned dangerous.

The tears continued to fall, making my vision blurry. I fiddled with my cell for a sec longer, knowing I had to do something and now. I stood up quickly and turned down the path, smacking hard into someone.

He *hmphed*, my forehead making sharp contact with a lean, muscled chest. I stumbled, my phone *clank-a-clackin'* to the ground, my hands coming up to grip the shirt of the person I'd slammed into.

Large hands landed on my upper arms, helping to steady me. "You okay?" The voice gave his identity away. Along with the spicy scent of his cologne.

The copper tint of blood filled my mouth and I realized I'd chomped down on my lip. "Think so," I replied, pressing my fingertips to the slight cut that seeped red, trying not to look up at Maurice.

I took a step back, but he followed, moving with me. One hand slid upward from my shoulder and cupped my cheek, his thumb swiping gently below my eye and catching up silver droplets.

"What's goin' on, Imani?"

He was standing close enough that I could feel the warmth of his breath as his husky voice broke into the silence. Unable to resist, I glanced up at his face. He was staring at me, not into my eyes but rather at the tears that had gathered on his fingers.

I stood quietly, absorbing the comfort of standing so closely, enjoying his heat, lost in the intensity of his look. My gaze dropped to his mouth, to perfect plump lips that last weekend had touched mine.

And then the tears welled again, and my bottom lip trembled at the memory. His dark brows came together, concern etched across his features. His hand stroked lower, his fingertips trailing lightly across my mouth.

He angled his head, came closer. "What is it, shortie?"

"Kayla." My hands curled into his Reggie Bush jersey.

"I heard you yellin'. What happened?"

"She's gone."

He looked confused. "Gone where?"

Shaking my head only helped a little bit, my thoughts muffled by his nearness. "Arizona."

"With her parents?"

"No, they went to Alaska on a cruise. Kayla met a guy online and I think she went to meet him."

"On GettinHooked?"

I nodded. "It's all hella jacked up. There's people from all over, just like MySpace."

"I noticed."

"Now Kayla—" I released his shirt and stepped

away quickly so his hands fell. I was straight trippin, lost my damn mind, standing here diggin' Maurice's closeness and touch when my cousin could be gettin' raped and murdered.

I shook my head, trying to gather my thoughts, completely stunned how easily I could be distracted by this hella fine boy. He did something juiced to me, but I could not allow my reaction to him to overshadow what I had to do to protect Kayla. To get her home safely.

"I gotta go." I turned, skipping out of his reach as I attempted to move around him and head for home.

"Wait, Imani," he said, grabbing my shirt to stop me. "Whatcha goin' to do?"

Shrugging, I glanced back at him over my shoulder, then took in a shaky breath as the heat of a fresh flash of tears burned in my eyes. "I gotta go home and get stuff to go after her."

"How you goin' to do that?"

I paused, my breath suspended, the pulse rushing in my ears the only sound. I hadn't thought of that—hell, I could hardly think at all; all I wanted to do was go after her. To bring her back.

"I don't know." My voice cracked, sounding hella scratchy. "Maybe a bus." I'd be able to catch a flight for free if I called my daddy and had him book it. Forget that, no way would he allow me to fly off to another state looking for Kayla. He might call the authorities, but he wouldn't let me do it, that was for damn sure.

"I'll drive you."

Gettin' a lift home would save me about fifteen minutes and with night settling around me, I'd be happy to take the ride, my knees still feeling jiggly. I nodded. "You know where I'm at, right? It's not far."

"Nah, shortie, I don't just mean home. I meant after Kayla. To Arizona."

I shook my head, thinking right quick how hella hard it'd be to spend so much time alone with him, being so close and remembering how we'd kissed, and knowing, too, that he'd probably banged Brie. "It's far," I whispered.

"I know, but Imani, I can't letcha go alone." He put up his hand, already knowing I was about to dispute his right to be telling me what I can and can't do, with or without him. "It's not like that, girlie. I'm not tryin' to boss ya, but I gotta look out for mines."

Mines? There he was, puttin' down some sorta claim again, but there was something sweet and tender in his voice, something intimate about the two of us standing alone in the darkness.

And with my brain hella foggy from lack of sleep, from fear and from the heat of his touch and gentle caress of his gaze, I was straight trippin', close to agreeing with whatever baby-boy said.

I nodded. Riding with Maurice would be safer than taking a bus, not to mention hexa faster and more comfortable. Not only that, it made more sense I not go alone considering that was exactly my fear for Kayla. "Your momma will let you?"

He grinned, flashin' me a pair of dimples. "I'll work it out." He tilted his head toward his place. "Lemme grab some shit and we can bounce."

"Aiight."

His hand slid down my shoulder to take mine and I dropped into step beside him.

CHAPTER 14

I let us into the condo, feelin' a little weird about bringin' him inside, unsure of what Gram would say to Maurice, about him being there. It was dark as usual, with just pale bluish light seeping into the front rooms from Gram's. Snoop was spittin' softly from my room.

I'd bounced outie so fast that I hadn't even bothered to turn off my stereo or power down the computer.

"Come here," I said, flickin' on a light and angling my head toward Gram's door, feelin' like I should intro Maurice to my Gram.

Maurice followed where I led without askin' questions or bein' asked twice, and I couldn't help grinning 'bout that even though the entire situation was whack. He'd changed out of sweats and into baggie faded Rocawear jeans while I'd waited in his car for him to get a few of his things. He looked hella good, his fade tight, rocks blinging on his ears, his smile ready and focused on me.

I shook my head, trying to quit peepin' 'im out and think about gettin' on the road. This was goin' to be frickin' hard, looking my Gram in the face and straight-up lying, but I had to. For Kayla.

I took a big breath and held it for a quick sec before letting it out crazy slow. Rappin' my hand against her door, I peeked inside just as her chair swiveled toward me. "Imani, baby, what is it?"

"Hey, Gram. I have someone here I want you to meet."

"Oh, okay, baby," she said, standing up and moving toward the door as I opened it farther. I knew when she caught her first glimpse of Maurice 'cause her eyes narrowed and her salt-and-pepper brows came together as her gaze landed on him.

"Who's your little boyfriend?" she asked, keeping her eyes on him, her face tilted up 'cause he was so much taller.

Nerves kept me from bustin' on her calling Maurice little, and I bit the inside of my cheek to keep from correcting her on the *boyfriend* thang. "Gram, this is Maurice Simms. Lives across from Kayla." I turned to him. "Maurice, my gram."

"Nice to meet you," he said, putting out his hand, his tone and gesture polite and fallin' into what Gram would expect.

"What you planning for Imani?" Gram's eyes remained

narrowed and fixed on him, her words laced with suspicion. "She don't mess with no boys, not you, either."

I coughed. "Gram, I'm not messin' with Maurice.
He's just a friend. He's giving me a lift to Kayla." I pur-
posely left off mentioning her crib since I was tryin' to
be vague enough to shade the lies.

But here came the biggie. "You're all right here on
your own for a few days, aren'tcha, Gram? I'm gonna
get a few thangs and hang with Kayla for a few days
while her parents are out of town. Is that cool with
you?" Had it been any one of my other girls, she'd have
suggested having 'em stay here with us while their
parents were gone. She wouldn't do that with Kayla,
so I was chill there.

"I'm grown, Imani. Don't need you babysitting me."
She replied. Her gaze drifted slowly off Maurice,
catching my eyes right quick before her gaze drifted
back to him. "He's not staying there, too, is he?"

My cheeks burned hella hot. "No, Gram, he's not
stayin' at Kayla's.

"Well, all right, baby. You don't get in no trouble." She
gave me a slight embrace, and I held her tight, guilt eating
an ugly dark hole in my gut. I hated lying to her, and there
was this little naggin' feeling that she already knew.

I kissed her cheek as she shifted back into her room,
her attention leaving me as she focused on Maurice.
"Don't be getting my baby into no mess, you hear?"

"Yes, ma'am."

Nah, Maurice hadn't caused the mess.

I had.

Gram shook her head, her slight shoulders looking more frail than usual, her eyes watering slightly from the light. Without saying anything else, she moved farther into her room and eased the door mostly closed again.

Grippin' my bottom lip between my teeth, I steadied my breaths and tried to get rid of the heat stainin' my cheeks, but kept my eyes averted from Maurice.

After a quick sec, I gathered myself and glanced up at him, to find him staring at me all hexa intensely. I cleared my throat, then kept my voice low so Gram wouldn't hear. "She's always warnin' me ta stay away from fellas. That was easy compared."

He chuckled. "My dad's the same. Always says girls are a path to trouble." He grinned a hella wicked smile that made his dimples deepen, then leaned close so he could whisper in my ear, "Makes sure I carry caps."

I jerked away from him too damn fast and smacked the back of my head on the door frame, a spark of pain on my scalp accompanied a shiver that flashed across my skin. I knew the caps he was talkin' 'bout were condoms, not the bottle kind. "Um...um...lemme get some stuff."

I moved past him, farther into the shadows of the hallway and toward my room where Ne-Yo sang his heart out on the radio. I felt him move behind me, his footfalls silent on the thick carpeting.

"Imani? Am I allowed back here?"

I knew what he was asking. Was I allowed to have him in my room and did I want him following. Had my daddy been at the skizouse there's no way Maurice would even be within ten feet of my room, but Daddy wasn't here and Gram was back in her room with the door closed.

Besides, nothing was going to happen between us, though I was still workin' over the condom comment in my brain. I wasn't a bopper, but I was pretty damn sure that Maurice knew that and wouldn't be trying nothing or thinking he was gonna get something from me.

Snap, he'd be getting nothing I didn't wanna give, and I sure didn't give it up easy. And not to dudes who were playas. But straight up, there was really no harm allowin' him into my room. I was just gonna toss some stuff in my pack and then we'd be alone on the road for hours together.

"Sure, come on." I opened my door and clicked on a light as I kicked off my shoes.

He'd followed close enough that I could feel his heat and smell his cologne. Feelin' warm deep in my belly, I glanced at the bed, then steadied my breaths.

Walking away from him, I grabbed my pack and set it open on a chair, then started swooping items from around my room and shoving them inside. Maurice just kinda stood at the door, lookin' slightly outta place against the pink bedding and walls covered with my boo, Usher.

I couldn't help grinning as I watched him out of the corner of my eye as I pulled panties and a clean bra from my drawer. And I picked sexy stuff, too, just feeling the need to tease him a little as I waved them around before they landed inside the canvas bag.

After going into the connecting bathroom and swiping some junk from there that was also added to my backpack, I shoved my feet into different tennies and yanked a jacket outta my closet.

"Hey, do you need gas money?" I asked, unable to keep the tint of excitement from my voice. Drivin' off with Maurice hadn't been a planned thang, and it sure wasn't for a good reason, but I'd be straight lying if I didn't think it was kinda hot.

Muscular shoulders rolled with his slight shrug. "I got some scratch. If you have some, you should probably bring it. No tellin' how much we'll need."

"Fo' sho', I've got plenty." I moved to my desk and lifted my Visa card that my daddy kept well supplied with Benjamins. I had some cash, too, and snagged that out of my purse and transferred it all into the front pocket of the single bag I was taking.

"I need to check my e-mail and see if James has

replied." Flicking the mouse to fire up the computer out of sleep mode, I plopped down into the chair and scrolled over to my in-box, holdin' my breath that there'd be something from either Kayla or the dude she'd split for.

"That's Kayla's friend, right?"

"Yup."

"Anything?"

There was a frickin' ton of messages, most of them my girls wanting to get at my dudes, wanna-be-hooked folks from my Web site. I moved through them, lookin' at the addies, but didn't see a thing I needed to.

My chest burned and despite being kinda hyped on this trip now, the back of my eyes burned and my throat felt hella thick, tight with worry and emotion. "Nah, nada."

"You should print out James's contact info and do a MapQuest to the campus."

"Good thinking." I converted info to printable files, then sent it to my Epson.

He'd moved in close, and knelt behind me. "See, shortie, I'm good for something."

When he spoke the warm wash of his breath caressed my skin, scurrying down my back. I shivered slightly, than glanced over my shoulder into his dark shimmering eyes.

He was so close that with a little lean I could have closed the distance and kissed him. To keep from doing it, I bit my lip again, and half smiled. "Drive me there, and I guess we'll see just how good for somethin' ya are."

I'd meant it to be teasin' but instead it sounded hella serious and kinda sexual, the way his gaze kept lingerin' on my mouth, followed by the way he licked his lips like I wanted to.

"All gravity, baby girl, I'll get you there."

His words felt so good I think I kinda half moaned when I sighed out a little breath.

There was somethin' else I had to do before we bounced. "Can you take my stuff done to your car? I wanna say goodbye to my Gram."

"Fa sheezy." He looked at me right quick, then brushed a couple wild ringlets of my crazy-ass curls off my forehead and tucked them behind my ear. He started pushing off his knees to get to his feet, but paused halfway up, leaning toward me; his mouth touched the skin, right where his fingertips had been a second before.

The contact was light and quick, but hella tender, too. When he stood up all the way he was grinning wide, but turned away fast, swiped the papers from the printer and swooped my pack, zippin' it up as he walked toward my bedroom door. "Aiight, I'll be waitin' in the ride for ya."

I hadn't realized I'd been holding my breath till he quit

the room and my chest started burning. Lettin' the whoosh of air escape my lungs, I turned back to my computer and clicked through pages until I was at Darian's. A couple more clicks, I was in his contact page, my fingers shakin' hella bad as I thought over my message.

I fo' sho' hadn't made the boy any promises and no damn commitments, but since I had teased him at the pallay—*and* kissed him—there was just somethin' in me that felt it only right to let the boy off the hook. I just couldn't think 'bout going off with one guy when another maybe thought he'd be startin' somethin' up with me.

Not a benda, and not a playa, either, I had to pick a guy, and if I was admittin' shit, I'd say that deep down I'd already chose. Darian never stood a chance.

And even with his "baby-girl," "shortie," and "mines" nicknames, Maurice hadn't said squat about me being his girl.

Steadying my fingers, I typed, "Hey Darian, please don't be mad, but the chillin' thang isn't gonna work out. You're hot though, boy, and beezies will be linin' up to talk to you. Hope you understand. Pixx Imani."

Hitting Send felt kind of liberatin', like a weight off my shoulders. No matter what happened with me and Maurice, I knew in my heart that Darian wasn't the guy for me, that he wasn't meant to be my prom date and it was best to nip it now before he felt I was leadin' him on.

My body shook slightly as I stood, my nerves jittering through my system; then, glancin' around my space, I peeped out everything to make sure I hadn't forgotten somethin' important.

When I was sure I hadn't, I took a deep breath and walked out the door. It was time to step, time to meet Maurice in the car.

CHAPTER 15

"Imani."

I heard my name through the fog of sleep, rich and low and whispered close to my ear.

"Imani? Wake up."

Slowly his voice intruded on my dreams and I became away of the cool glass pressed against my forehead and the seat belt keeping me from completely slumpin' over in the seat.

"Hmm?" I turned slowly in the seat and opened my eyes.

"You know how to drive, shortie?"

Rubbing my palm against my eyes, I wiped away the remaining sleep and took in the sight of Maurice, his face illuminated only by the pale green light coming from the dash. He'd removed his zip-up jacket and now just wore a Tupac T-shirt, some bling encrusted into the cotton settin' off the rocks heavy on his earlobes.

His gaze was intent, but tired. The whites of his eyes a little bloodshot.

"How to drive?"

"Yeah, can you drive?"

I shook my head. Hella lame, I know, but I've always been kinda afraid to learn. "No."

He sighed and I saw his shoulders slump some. "Don't be mad, girl, but we have to stop. I need some sleep."

And I could hear it in his voice, too. In the way he sagged in his seat.

For the first time, I pulled my gaze off his hexa cute face and glanced out the blackened reflective window. We'd pulled off Interstate 5 and were parked in a parking lot. An Exxon station was across the street, a Burger King's neon sign blinkin' on the car window, along with an entrance to a Holiday Inn.

"Where are we?"

"Just a little south of Bakersfield."

"Oh." We'd been driving a lot longer than it felt. Once we'd stepped from my condo, we'd filled his car with gas and picked up some pops and water for the ride. By the time we hit the highway, it'd been nearly nine o'clock. Glancing at the digital clock on his stereo, I saw it was now pushing two.

I sat up a little in my seat. "I didn't realize we'd been drivin' so long."

His hand touched my cheek, his thumb gently smoothing across my lips. "You fell asleep pretty quick."

I felt heat on my cheeks and was thankful for the darkness so he couldn't see the pink stains taint my skin. "Sorry."

He smiled. "You're cute asleep. Nibble on your lip sometimes, it's sexy as hell."

I grinned back, the pink turnin' downright red as warmth uncurled down my spine. He'd been really looking to notice my habit of sucking on my lips in my sleep. I guess hella better than snorin' or grinding teeth.

"Were you watching the road at all?"

He laughed. "Not really."

"Oh." I hadn't expected him to admit checkin' on me as he drove. "You wanna get a room?" I asked to change the subject but it just deepened the intensity of his expression.

After a sec he said, "If you're uncomfortable, we can just sleep in the car for a minute. I can't drive farther tonight, though, Imani. You chill with that?"

"Yeah, I know. You're tired." I looked at the hotel, the long two-story building was sportin' hella rows of windows, each a room. "If we sleep here and leave in the morning, how long do you think before we hit 'Zona?"

He shrugged. "I think we're 'bout halfway, but I'm not sure. I'd say by afternoon."

"Aiight." Releasing my belt, I reached into the backseat and grabbed my backpack, then opened the door to step out. "A telly it is."

Maurice didn't say anything as he left the car, hit the alarm on his key entry remote, then came to my side. We walked together through the dimly lit parking lot toward the Holiday Inn.

At this time of night the lobby was all locked up and registration was a tiny little whack window, with a bell to let the attendant know we were there. It took a hella long time to rouse an older woman to come to the window to help us out.

She was eyeing us all suspicious-like when she asked, "What do you need?"

Um...what the—? I felt like askin' for a cheeseburger or a Slurpee, 'cause come on, we were at a hotel. How dumb did the woman have to be not to know we wanted a room? I kept my mouth shut, though. I was hella frickin' grouchy and I didn't want the bootch to send us away.

"We need a room," Maurice replied before I could.

"ID and credit card."

He took out his ID and plopped it on the counter, sliding it under the low window. "Can I pay cash?"

"I have my card." I bent to fiddle in the front pocket of my pack. Retrieving the Visa my daddy kept full of grip, I put it on the counter.

The woman picked up both, her stare steady as she held both cards next to each other, then turned her narrowed eyed glare on us. "You're not old enough to get a room."

A heavy hand landed on my shoulder, Maurice's strong fingers drawing a slow circle on my upper back. "We're married."

I stopped breathing, and shit, I think my heart jammed up, too, but I kept my face emotionless, working hard to not show my surprise.

"The names aren't the same," she replied, angling the ID and Visa our way to indicate what she was talking about.

"It hasn't been long 'nough to fix that."

His hand had slid from my upper back, down my side and now rested lazily on my hip, his fingers creeping up and touchin' skin below the hem of my shirt. Looping his thumb into my pants, he scooted me a little closer, but kept his hand in place even when there was no frickin' gap between us.

After a sec, the woman nodded and started typing into her computer. "Is the address correct?" she asked. Maurice kept on dealin' with her, but their words faded out as my pulse rushed hella loud in my ears.

We were gettin' a room and in a quick sec we'd be handed the key. So I stood there at Maurice's side as the attendant swiped my card and had me sign, though I had a straight-up hard time moving, my knees hecka tremblin' and my hands shaking as I signed the slip.

I mean, dayum, I was gettin' a room with a dude.

A few more minutes and Maurice had his hand linked with mine, his warm palm pressed tightly against my skin, his fingers laced between mine.

I dropped into step beside him as he guided us to our room, then slid the thin plastic card into the lock and opened the door.

The room was dark aside from a small light on the wall in the bathroom, which was to our immediate right. I heard Maurice touch the wall a couple times, then golden light flooded the room and hurt my eyes after being in the dark for so long.

"There's just one bed," I commented, my gaze fixed on the big bed settin' smack against the wall and takin' up most of the small room.

"I told her we were hooked up, I couldn't exactly ask for two beds."

"Yeah, I know." Aww, lawdy, I wish the lights were back off right quick, so he wouldn't be able to see my face. And I wouldn't be able to see the bed.

"You cool?"

I nodded but didn't say anything as I untangled our fingers and moved deeper into the room, droppin' my backpack on a chair by the TV. It'd been years since

I'd traveled with my daddy, but we'd always stayed in much nicer hotels, nothing roadside like this one.

The room was nice enough, but it hella reminded me of the tricks at school who rented telly rooms to spread 'em for their fellas. Or whatever fella wanted a piece of coochie, because give-it-up girls were like that.

Finding the remote to the TV, I flicked it on. When light filtered off the set, Maurice clicked off the overhead lamp and walked toward the bed, then pulled back the blankets and sat down.

He didn't say anything as he shrugged out of his shirt, tossed it to the chair where my bag was. A minute later I heard the *clink-clank* of his belt and it slid from his jeans as he fiddled with the button fly, then bent forward to untie his shoes.

The entire time I stood staring at his muscular back, his dark skin smooth and rich-looking, set off by the pale milky colors coming off the TV program. He was gettin' naked and I couldn't think to move or kick off my own shoes or lose my sweatshirt.

With my damp palms pressed to my thighs, I shook my head, tryin' hella hard to snap out of it, to shut my mouth 'cause I was trippin' gaping at him. Licking my lips, I tried to get myself together before he noticed.

Takin' a couple deep breaths, then letting 'em out slowly, I squeezed my lids closed tight. When not lookin' at him I was able to turn away.

When I opened my eyes, Maurice had turned on the bed and was smiling at me, one dark brow arched and the twin dimples dancing on his cheeks. He'd slid one leg beneath the comforter, which made the denim V of his pants spread, givin' me a peep at his boxers beneath.

"All gravity?" he asked, leaning back on one elbow and pulling his other leg up onto the bed.

He was going to sleep with his jeans on, I realized, glad that the only light in the room was from the TV.

"Gravy." I smiled, kicked off my shoes, tossed my sweatshirt, and climbed into the bed, turning on my side facing him and tuckin' the pillow so it was sorta between us. "You want the TV off?"

"Mmm-hmm…" His voice was trailin' off, all soft and hexa sexy sounding. Shoving down the plump of the pillow with a fist, I looked at his face and saw that his eyes were already closed. One arm was curled up beneath his head, showing off the thickness of his biceps.

Reachin' behind me, I found where I'd set the remote and shut off the set, sending the telly room into almost complete darkness. Through the thick drapes I could see the neon signs I'd seen from the parkin' lot and over the slow, even breathing of Maurice, I could hear cars on the freeway whizzin' by hella fast.

Just as I closed my eyes, Maurice's hand settled over mine on my pillow. His touch straight startled me, 'cause I'd been sure he'd already drifted off.

"Hey, Imani?" His voice was low and all sleepy.

"Yeah," I whispered.

"Whatcha fight with Kayla 'bout?"

"I wanted to shut down GettinHooked.com."

"Why?"

I sighed, turning my hand so we were palm to palm, his so much bigger than mine. "It was gettin' hella whack."

"Aww..."

The silence stretched again, his body still aside from the rise and fall of his bare chest and I was pretty sure he'd finally fallen asleep. Leavin' my hand beneath his, I tried to settle into the bed, to relax into the mattress and not be so afraid we'd end up touchin' more.

My lids heavy, my lashes fallin' to my cheeks, I dreamily yawned, last night's lack of sleep takin' its toll and bringin' me down hard, the last of my energy seepin' out of every muscle.

And then his voice came in the darkness again, so softly I didn't get it all and wasn't sure if he was askin' a question or making a statement, and I was too tired to reason out his words, though they played over in my head as I drifted off... *"Imani, you don't need your site no more."*

CHAPTER 16

Maurice's hand was on my hip, his long fingers half on the jersey of my sweats, half on my skin under my shirt. And his soft lips were kissing me, on my cheeks, at the corners of my mouth, on the sensitive skin by my ear.

I didn't wanna open my eyes, didn't want to wake up and find out that I was dreaming and I was actually in my bed on the same short night I'd cried myself to sleep.

Just to peep out if he was real, I turned slightly onto my side toward him. Not daring to lift my lids, I lifted my hand and settled it on his chest.

His naked chest.

His muscles quivered under my fingertips and he made a little throaty noise that made me warm and gushy inside.

"Morning, shortie," he whispered, between raining kisses across my face.

I smiled. Okaaay, this was fo' sho' no dream. "Hi." My voice cracked a little, but he just chuckled and took advantage of my smile by planting his mouth full on mine and sweeping his tongue across my lips, then inside.

I let him kiss me, let him angle his head so his tongue stroked softly against mine, let him lead me until that warm gushy feelin' was hella on fire and all I could think 'bout was if he quit now I might cry. Or die. Or worse, beg him to start up with this mess again.

Oh, my lawdy, I straight up didn't even care about my morning breath, and he sure as hell didn't, either. He kissed me deep, pressing me back onto the firm mattress of the telly room, his large body half covering me.

Slowly his mouth moved from mine, smoothing tongue and lips down my jaw, then to my neck. His hand was hella set loose, roaming all free and crazy across my body, creepin' up beneath my shirt across my bare skin.

My thoughts skittered to my lack of bra, which lay on the floor, haphazardly discarded in the middle of the night.

His palm settled over my flesh, and I straight up couldn't help the nervous giggle. I turned more fully into him, breakin' off the kiss, and put my forehead to his chest. "We're in a room."

He made a sound at the back of his throat, but I felt it rumble up from his chest. "Yup, you chill with that?"

Hexa chill. I think. I'd kissed other guys. I'd made out with other fellas. This wasn't the first time I'd had a hand up my shirt, but it was the first time evah I was all up in a room, alone with a half-dressed hottie who was totally diggin' the kisses and feelin'.

I could tell.

And his whispered words did a ring-a-ding in my skull: *carry caps.* And I knew now, like I knew then, he'd meant condoms, and I hella wondered if he had some with him now. In the half craziness of sleep, I wanted this boy, wanted to go all the way, and I'd let him do it, too.

I nodded. And with the slight movement his hands went back to caressing me, back to roaming all free across my body, making my skin hella tingle.

"I'll quit if ya tell me," he mumbled, and his non-pressure made me feel way better about lettin' him continue.

I believed him. I believed that if I told him to stop he would, unlike some dudes I'd known 'bout, some situations my girls had gotten into.

Relaxin' into his touch, into his mouth and kisses, I ran my hand up his chest, over muscular shoulders, up the back of his neck and across the stubble of his clean fade. "I know."

"You done this before?"

"No." I didn't hesitate in my reply.

But he paused, his kisses stopping, his body going still half above me. And I heard his breathing change up, too. I wasn't ready for this to be over, wasn't ready for the warmth and softness to be cooled out if he was having second thoughts 'bout being with a virgin.

Putting my hand on the back of his head, I pulled his head down toward mine, and kissed him instead. And so he lost the stillness and went back to doin' what he had been that was makin' me feel light-headed, yet alive.

With each kiss the passing thoughts of him not even being my man faded out. Thoughts of prom dates and wannabe hook-ups. Of GettinHooked.com and all the trouble it'd caused. Not even the remainin' shaded bruise on my cheek mattered. Only feelin' fully what Maurice was doing to me.

And then his hand dipped straight up into my pants and I knew I didn't wanna stop him. Except…thoughts of Kayla crept into my head, and fear resurfaced. Hard.

Here I was, cup caking and playing cuddle-up with the guy I wanted so bad. I was safe and secure in his arms, doin' junk I'd never even wanted to do wit' no one else. Junk I wanted to keep on doin'. Because he was gentle and tender and makin' this all right. Makin' it right.

But Kayla, Kayla was out there with a stranger. For all I knew—she knew—James was a forty-year-old man with a thang for teen girls.

I was into Maurice. Pickin' up what he was layin' down. But Kayla could be being raped, or even murdered.

Even with Maurice's sweet kisses and tender caresses, tears welled behind my eyes. My throat tightened as I attempted to keep them at bay. But I failed and fat drops slipped off my lashes.

After a sec, Maurice must have tasted their saltiness mingled with our makin' out. His body still again, he lifted his head, his brows pulled together, his dark eyes intent on me when I lifted my lids and looked at him.

"You scared?" He touched my cheek, swipin' away some of the liquid stainin' my skin. "I said I'd stop. You shoulda told me."

I shook my head, my throat too tight to talk, my mouth too dry to form words. His warm palm cupped my cheek, his thumb gently stroked across my lips, and I could tell he was fightin' hella hard to get himself in check.

"You okay, Imani? I didn't wanna do shit you don't like."

"I like it," I croaked out, somehow forcing out the words, a sob startin' to bubble up.

He flashed this boyish grin that showed off his cutie-pie dimples. "What then, shortie?"

"Kayla." And then tears streamed out hexa fast and the sob I'd been holdin' back escaped. Feelin' hella dumb, I turned my face away and once again put my forehead to his chest so he couldn't see me cryin'.

He didn't nothing at first, just held me while I cried. Stroked his big hands down my back, pushed back unruly wild-ass curls from my face, now dampened by my fussin'.

"You're worried 'bout her."

I nodded.

His voice lowered, and I could feel the warmth of his breath brush against my ear. "Me, too."

I nodded again, but between sobs there wasn't much I could say. Wrappin' my arms around his back, I curled into him, absorbing his heat, totally comfortable sharin' this moment with him. In fact, it felt good to be there with him because usually I cried alone.

My daddy was gone when I needed him. I hated to burden Gram when I was upset, and I'd never had a momma to share this with. But Maurice was here, and oh, my lawdy, I needed him. Needed this from him as much as I needed and wanted the kisses and affection.

He held me, like I'd longed for someone to do. He let me cry, without offerin' up advice or judgment. With my cheek tight against his firm chest, I could feel his heart beat, the slow and steady rhythm hella soothin' when I was feelin whacked and out of it.

A bit of time must ticked off the clock because the

weepin' let up and I was able to make words again. Takin' a hecka big gulping breath, I lifted my head and leaned back so I could look at him.

"Maybe I'm trippin', but I'm worried 'bout her." I touched his chest where I'd left some nasty snot from all my boo-hooing. "I liked it, though. I'm not upset about the kissin' 'n stuff." My face heated.

"But I just got ta thinkin'. Here I am, all cuddled up with you, and feelin' hella good—" I watched him smile "—and it was safe and right, but K is out there with some guy she doesn't know. Some guy who may not be sweet like you are."

An eyebrow lifted, but a dimple danced. "I'm sweet?" And he kissed me hard with some added tongue to maybe prove he wasn't.

I was kinda breathless when he was through. "Yeah. Sweet. But you smellin' me about Kayla?"

He nodded. "So let's step then. The sooner we bounce, the sooner we'll get there."

"Fa shizzle."

"You wanna shower?"

Heat pumped up all crazy onto my cheeks again, thinkin' I'd be gettin' for real naked in the next room, even though I was about to get down in the bed with him a few secs ago. "Yup."

He rolled outta the bed, leavin' me feelin' all hella cold and lonely and wishing right quick that we could forget about the rest of the world and go back to makin' out.

For a moment I just lay there watching him, his brown skin lookin' rich and smooth in the dimness of our room. The fly on his jeans gaped open and the denim clung all low on his hips.

His body moved powerfully across the room to where I'd dumped my pack, then with a wink he swooped it up and carried it to the bathroom. A sec later I heard the shower turn on, the water smackin' down on the tub.

"All ready. You go first," he said, walkin' out of the bathroom.

Rightin' my shirt and sweats under the covers, I got out of the bed, my heart thumpin' hella hard. For a quick minute there, I thought he'd meant to shower with me.

"Thanks." I reached up and kissed his cheek as I went by, steppin' into the bathroom, then my head hexa debatin' on whether or not to lock the door. I ended up not. Let what happens happen, I was feelin' all ready for the next step with Maurice.

But he didn't come in. I showered pretty quickly, knowing the water and telly soap would help out the puffiness of my cried-out eyes, and make me fresh and ready to face the rest of the day.

I dressed in the bathroom, too, then swapped with Maurice. He showered while I combed my hair and put on my socks and sneakers.

Less than an hour after full-on makin' out then breakin' into tears, we gathered all our stuff and pixxed out.

Time to find Kayla.

CHAPTER 17

The highway sped by. After we left the L.A. area, the highway turned into mile after mile of nothin' much, spreadin' into even hecka less. The scope of the low hills and desert was hella different than the city streets of the Bay Area, or even the smooth lanes and courts of the suburbs just outside The Bay, where I lived.

Maurice and I didn't talk much as we moved down the long stretch of road, the bright sun seepin' in through his tinted windows. Mac Dre was on his CD player right now, like most of the ride we just listened to the music and let the hours tick by.

But it was a comfortable silence, one filled with hand-holdin' and soft, tender smiles that made me feel like I was the most special girl in the world. And there were times that I'd glance his way and his warm eyes were fixed on me rather than the road. Somethin' in his gaze made me want a replay of the telly. Want another chance to play cuddle-up, to be in his arms again.

And I'd grin back at him, gigglingly point to the road, so that his dimples would get all deep before he pulled his gaze from me to be checkin' on drivin' again.

There was somethin' straight intimate about being alone on the road with him, on our own, like a team; Maurice and me against the world. Or at least the crazos of the Internet.

We'd only stopped once, to fill his tight ride with gas and to find some food. We found a small rest stop, complete with a few gas stations and our choice of a run for the border or Denny's. We opted for burritos and ate them in the car, talkin' and laughin' before we hit the road again.

When we crossed out of Cali, I couldn't help the hella nervous coil of fear that wound all crazy tight in my gut. The tension caused my hands to tremor, but Maurice tightened his fingers around me and offered up reassurance. "We're gonna find her," he said, and if he hadn't been behind the wheel, I'd have kissed him for sayin' so.

After heading south on 17 for a few hours, I could feel the tension start to build for a second time. Now the ride was drawing to an end as the hella empty sand and dirt turned green as we neared towns and populated areas.

When we passed Cave Creek Recreation Area, we decided it was time to find a place to pull off the highway and try to figure out where we were goin' next. When we stepped from the car the air was hella warmer than The Bay, and dry, too.

I stretched my legs for a sec, then reached into the backseat and found my pack. Searchin' inside, I swooped the info I'd printed off about James and dialed his number on my cell.

With Akon in the background as his ring tone, James told me to leave a message. At least he sounded young, and not forty-somethin', I thought as I smashed my thumb to disconnect the call. Then redialed, just hexa hoping the fella would pick up.

And he did. "Wassup?"

"James?"

"Yeah, who wants to know?"

My heart was hella thump-a-thumpin', my hand shakin' as I held the phone. For a right quick sec, my eyes blurred over in relief, and through the fuzz of liquid, I saw Maurice step in my direction with his hand outstretched, like he was tryin' to help me.

I cleared my throat. "Um...this is Imani. I'm Kayla's cousin. You know Kayla?"

He didn't say a thang, but I could hear him shuffle around on the other end of the line, could hear muffled voices murmurin' somethin'.

"Yeah, I know Kayla. Why do you want to know?"

My knees were shakin' now, and I slid back into the

Altima onto the plush seat inside. Maurice squatted before me, his hand settled on my hip, his look questioning.

"Can I talk to her for a sec?" My voice cracked, and I wondered why I was hella stupid enough to have been trippin' so bad that I hadn't tried to dial them both over and over again since we'd left home.

"Not right now."

"Why!" I knew I yelled, but I hexa couldn't help it. I was freakin'. I wanted to act like I was two again, and have a full-out temper tantrum with foot stompin' and screamin'. I wanted to know why they hadn't bothered respondin' to any of my desperate messages.

He laughed. "She's in the bathroom." He cleared his throat, then added, "Shower."

"Oh."

"Whatcha think, I killed her or something?"

Or raped her. Or had her tied up. Or somethin' else nasty and awful. Fo' sho', that's what I thought—the guy hadn't done a thang to make me think otherwise.

Now that I knew she was safe—mostly—anyway, the fear was hella getting swapped with being pissed. Hella frickin' PO'd.

My cheeks flamed, with anger and maybe just a tad with being caught up in all the drama hype the media creates when teens get lured away by the 'net. Hell, I was in 'Zona because of my Web site.

"Yup, I guess."

"Nah, she's fine. Want me to have her ring ya?"

"Hey, James?"

"Huh?"

"Um, actually…I'm in Arizona. Near Phoenix. Can you tell me where y'all are at and we'll come there?"

"*We'll?* Ya didn't bring her folks did ya?"

"No, I'm with—" I broke off and glanced at Maurice, *my boyfriend* nearly drippin' like rain from my tongue. But I wasn't his girl, and despite him bein' here, and all the rubbin' up we'd done in the room, he hadn't said shit about us bein' a couple. I cleared my throat. "My friend drove me."

"Aiight. You got something to write with?"

I dug into my pack and got prepped for him to lay down the info we needed to find my girl and make sure she was safe.

After he gave us directions to the campus of Arizona State that he went to and lived on, I said, "Later." Then clicked my phone shut, feelin' this weird release.

"What up?" Maurice asked, still crouched in the gap of the open car door in the V of my legs in front of me. "He's a peanut?"

"He sounds cool, actually." I realized maybe I was wrong to have freaked the way I had over him, but still in my heart I knew I was right about needin' to shut down GettinHooked.com. As off the chain as the idea had been, without some sorta security system, the entire concept was way outta pockets now. And dangerous.

"But he wouldn't let you talk to Kayla?"

I shook my head. "She's in the shower."

He grinned, then lifted a brow. I wasn't stupid. I knew what they'd been doing—or at least I had a pretty good idea. And Maurice knew, too, I could tell by the way he peeped me out, with his eyes all glossy and a soft curve to his full, yummy lips.

I knew he was thinking 'bout our close encounter the night before.

"Um, I think we're still a bit away. His school is in Tempe." I waved the paper I'd scribbled on. "He gave directions. Let's bounce."

Maurice nodded but didn't move right away. He kept lookin' at me, like there was somethang else he wanted to say. I touched his face, my touch light at first, then I traced his lips with my fingertips and wondered what it was that was thick on his brain.

Then some tension eased from his body and his breath released warm across my skin. He rose, leaned forward and kissed me full on the lips, just with the slightest hint of tongue sliding all sexi-like across me.

"You did good, shortie," he said, with a devilish wink. Another quick peck to my mouth and he backed away and rounded the car, sliding behind the wheel.

There was nothin' I could say, 'cause I wasn't really

sure what I'd done good at. Instead I felt like I hella lost it. I was in 'Zona for spring break, chasing after Kayla, who'd lost her head and chased after some boy.

Maurice took the directions I'd jotted down and peeped them over right quick, before putting his car into gear and getting back on the road.

As we eased closer into Phoenix, the neighborhoods started lookin' familiar, almost, like suburbs that could be dropped into any place in the States with very little differences. The houses looked to be 'bout the same age as mine, 'bout the same size and style, too, as the one that littered all the places popppin' up around The Bay.

There were differences, too, and surprises. The air was much stiller here, and lacked the damp scent of salt and sea life that sprayed up from the Pacific. Livin' near the ocean fo' sho' gave off its own scent. Nothin' like the dry smell of the middle of the desert.

But there were a hella lot of palm trees and that threw me. I didn't expect them out here, but rather in L.A. or a tropical isle.

I think it was the palm trees that struck me most as we neared the Tempe campus of Arizona State, following the directions James had given.

Just as he'd done for much of the ride, Maurice's warm fingers were wrapped around mine, and he gave me a little squeeze, then stroked his thumb across my palm. "We're here."

"I'm scared." It's not what I meant to say, but it came out anyhow.

"We found her, Imani. You said James didn't sound bad."

"I know." And I did, but still I couldn't shake the tingle of apprehension tap-dancing down my spine. "But what if she doesn't wanna come back with us? What if she's so wound up that...that..."

"Hey, nah, baby-girl." He winked and a dimple appeared in his cheek. "She'll know it's time to go."

I tried to force a smile, but it was faulty. "I'm still scared."

He brought our joined hands to his mouth, his gaze driftin' from drivin' to my eyes all tender as he kissed my fingers right quick. "Don't be. I'm here, Imani. I got your back, you feelin' me, right?"

"Yup." And I guess I did, too. He hadn't said shit about it before, but then he was here. He was here for me when so few had ever been. And just havin' him here did help lighten up the fear that squeezed hexa tight around my lungs, makin' it hard to breathe.

My eyes teared. I think a few escapee droplets of salty liquid may have escaped my lower lashes, but I turned away from Maurice, slid the window down and let the air rush into the car, across my face, drying up the trails before a thang could be made 'bout 'em.

It wasn't long before the Sun Devil signs were

poppin' up all around us and Phoenix gave way to the college campus. We skirted the campus, followin' the directions James had given to find the dorms.

We pulled into a parkin' lot that was more empty than full, spots sprinkled everywhere, I guess since it was spring break and hella folks probably went home or on vacation during the recess from classes.

Maurice finally pulled in between an empty set of white lines, then put his tight ride into park, turnin' off the ignition.

I reluctantly released Maurice's hand, his touch offerin' up so much reassurance, then opened the door and stepped from the car. My gaze drifted across the 'scape around me, taking in the lines of palms, the buildings that reminded me of old Spanish movies, sets created as backdrops for adventures, and the more modern cement walks that led away from the lot, wondering which direction to find James's dorm.

Takin' a deep breath of warm, dry air, I closed the door and moved away from the car, turnin' toward Maurice. That's when I saw her. It was the long blond hair that gave her away. The golden strands danced on the breeze behind her as she ran my direction.

"Kayla!"

CHAPTER 18

I **couldn't** quit huggin' her. And doin' this crazy-ass mix of laughin' and cryin'. Kayla was doing it, too, I could hear her mumbled sobs swirled up in her giggles. I could feel it in the way her body trembled and in the way her thin arms wound about my back and hung on.

After a drug-out minute, we released, steppin' back a bit, but still linking our arms.

"I can't believe you came all this way," she said, shifting her blue-eyed gaze from my face over to Maurice. I saw the sparkle in their sky-colored depths and as she swiped a few fresh tears from her cheek, I also saw the knowing smile.

"I had to come after ya."

She lowered her voice. "With Maurice?"

My cheeks hella heated, and I knew my eyes were givin' everything away. She could read me like a book, and I knew right then she'd know how strong I felt about the boy.

Her brows rose, her grin widening. She whispered in my ear, but even the whisper was loud enough for Maurice to hear. "With Maurice," she repeated.

"He offered to drive me." I couldn't look at him right then, because my face felt like it was on fire. Shrugging, I tried to make it seem casual, though the secret was straight-up outed already. I had to hella fight the need to glance behind me to catch the look on his face.

"You came all this way?"

"Uh, yeah, girl, and so did you." I backed away a bit, relief at seeing her safe giving way to how pissed I was that she'd taken off and I'd had to fly after her.

"You didn't have to come."

"Yeah, I did." I lowered my voice, tryin' hard to keep my cool. "How'd you get here, anyway?"

"A bus."

"You took a bus? All this way?"

She laughed lightly. "Yeah, and it took a hella long time, too. At least you had Maurice to drive you."

"You took a bus to a boy who coulda been a killer or rapist."

She pushed back a few long strands from her face, a few remained locked on her eyelashes. "James is cool."

"But K, you couldn't have been so sure." I did look

at Maurice now, hoping to get him to affirm what I was sayin'. He nodded, and I fought the need to smile. "He coulda been anybody, any sort of nasty old man who couldn't wait to get you away from home."

"But he's not."

"But he coulda been."

"But he's not."

I grabbed her upper arms in both hands and gave her a little shake. I couldn't help it. All this winding, building emotion of the last few days, of first arguing with her, then finding her skippin' joint, then being on the road with the fella that made my heart race and skin burn, all the way to being here in the parking lot of ASU and findin' her safe. It was too much, and my body was startin' to trip.

Tremblin', I shook her again. "Don'tcha get it, K? He coulda killed ya. Don'tcha see how bad this coulda gone down?"

"Iman—"

"No! I was scared ta death. You shouldn't have done this. And it's my fault, too, just because I wanted Maurice."

Kayla's eyes went all big, then shimmered with amusement as she glanced from my face to the guy standin' beside me. Maurice.

Snap. Lawdy, had I just really said that aloud? Had I just really confessed what the entire Gettin' Hooked

Web site was all about? Until now, not even Kayla had known about my motives.

Squeezing my lids closed, I fought the flames lickin' mischief across my cheeks and dancing down my spine. My hands loosened their grip from her arms and slid slowly to my sides.

The *thump-a-thump* of my heartbeat was ringin' loud in my ears.

"Why didn't you tell me, girlie?" I felt Kayla tuck some of my wild curls behind my ear, but I could hear the laughter in her voice even when her touch was lovin'.

Then a stronger hand replaced hers and I was turned into the wall of a larger body. Maurice's. His arms came around me, tuckin' me close into his embrace.

"All this was for me?" he whispered softly to my ear, his warm breath seepin' into my soul.

I nodded, but hadn't found the will to open my eyes yet. The secret was out, no denyin' it now, I guess. It'd have been hexa faulty to come up with a lame-ass excuse.

He made this sexy-as-hell noise in his chest, then kissed the sensitive skin along my neck. I was shakin' again, my whole body tremblin'.

"Is she cryin'?" Kayla stroked affectionately down my back. "Imani, I'm okay. James is a good guy."

I nodded again, tryin' to overcome the feelin' of

Maurice's touch and concentrate on what Kayla was saying. My fists tightened into the T-shirt Maurice was wearing and I could feel the firmness of his muscular back beneath.

Touchin' him like this made it hard to think about being in 'Zona. Hard to think about the chase after Kayla. Hard to think at all.

"Don't be mad, girl. I shoulda told you my plan." Kayla was still rubbing my shoulders and I knew she thought all the quiverin' I was doing was 'bout her.

As hard as it was, I released Maurice and stepped away a bit, keepin' my gaze from strayin' to his. Despite the way he held me, kissed me, touched me, stroked me, he still didn't say fo' sho' if he wanted to claim me.

"Do you see now, K? Do you see how dangerous GettinHooked.com is?"

She shrugged, but didn't seem to take it to heart. Instead, she glanced over her shoulder, and for the first time I noticed there was a dude standing a few yards off, kinda lingerin' back a bit, lettin' our scene play out.

"James isn't dangerous, Imani." She ushered him over with a few waves of her hand. "Meet him and you'll see."

Okay, true, maybe James *wasn't* dangerous, but she didn't know that when she skipped out on me.

As I turned to face the fella who'd lured my cousin from home, I felt solid, warm fingers twine with mine, in a slightly possessive way. He kinda stepped forward, too, so he was slightly in front of me.

James was as cute in person as he had been in the crapload of pics Kayla had printed off his profile. A light-skinned brothah with hazel eyes and an athletic body. He seemed shy, or quiet. Or maybe he knew I was pissed and wasn't quite ready to deal with this hot-off chick yet.

He lifted his chin, his gaze glossin' over each of us. "What up?"

"Whatitdo," replied Maurice, playin' bodyguard as he kept me tucked behind him.

I could feel Kayla's eyes burnin' my back, and knew she was peepin' what was goin' down with Maurice and me.

She cleared her throat. "James, my cousin, Imani. Imani, this is James. And my friend, Maurice. Maurice, James."

The two guys gave each other a manly hand pound, Maurice makin' a gruff sound as he added, "Hey."

I could tell Kayla was nervous 'bout this confrontation, but so long as James was cool, she didn't need to be. "I'm starved, Kayla. Can we find someplace to eat?"

Maurice laughed. "We ate burritos hella long ago. I could use some food, too."

Kayla stepped toward James and grasped his hand the same way Maurice had mine. "Can you show us around campus, then find us a place to grub?"

"Walkin' would be good. We've been sittin' in my ride for hours." Maurice rolled his shoulders. "I need'a move around some."

"I'm feelin' ya." He angled his head and moved off in that direction. "Sure thang."

After a right quick sec, we all fell into place and followed, slowly making our way across campus. When we first started steppin', James told us about Irish Hall, the two-story gray building that housed his dorm. How the community bathrooms worked, and about the computer lab he'd used to find Gettin-Hooked.com.

I couldn't help flashing my gaze at Kayla as she walked hand-in-hand with James. If he'd found our site here, no tellin' how many other beezies and skeezies had found it, too. Lawdy, our numbers were growin' like mad, and it was crazy clear that it wasn't all high schoolers, and no doubt, not just a local thang no more.

James was sprinklin' as we walked, all about the campus and events held here. He told us about the huge circular building we'd seen as we'd driven to the parking structure: the Grady Gammage Memorial Auditorium, a hexxa tight site, surrounded by water.

But we moved in the opposite direction, James soon spittin' facts about Sun Devil Stadium and the athletics program that had recruited him from his Chicago high school for a football scholarship.

But football season being over, it didn't take long before Maurice and James were talkin' 'bout hoopin', school stats and their fave pro teams and players. Ballin' was Maurice's thang, and I could feel his excitement and energy as he talked 'bout it seep through his hand.

Despite the surreal feelin' that was pumpin' through my body, it was all gravity being here. Things were chill for now, Kayla was safe, Maurice was by my side and I thought I'd made a little dent on my cousin about the dangers of our Web site.

With the warm sun beatin' down on and my hair driftin' on the gentle breeze, my thoughts turned away from worry, to just doin' the do and bein' in the moment. It was cool seeing Kayla's smiles and hearin' her laughter.

I listened silently as Maurice and Kayla filled James in on Frisco and livin' in the Bay Area. Since Mac Dre had spread his hyphie movement all 'bout, James knew some of the smack we talked about, which had me grinnin' when he said things in his Chicago accent.

But the same words had Kayla blushin' and her bright blue eyes goin' all shiny. Made me wonder what happened between the two of them during the time she'd been one upped on our chase behind her. When we got a sec alone, I'd ask her about it.

For now? I glanced around. To Kayla and James

walkin' holdin' hands. To Maurice, who was connected to mine, too. And realized we looked as much like a couple as my cousin did with her fella. And I couldn't help the knotted-up feelin' in my gut that in addition to talkin' to Kayla about her relationship, I was gonna need to take a right quick peep at my own.

What was up with Maurice and me? Was he playin' me because we were alone on the road and I was convenient? Was there more? He hadn't been down with Darian kissing me. But had that been the male ego thang, or somethin' more?

My thoughts were interrupted by a tug on my hand. We'd changed directions, and I'd been all caught up and hadn't noticed. When I looked up, Maurice was lookin' at me all funny-like, his dark eyes questionin' and his brows pulled together some.

"You cool?" he asked, his voice low and intended just for me. The concern laced in his tone stroked against somethin' intimate inside me.

Warmth uncurled through my body, and my heart rate picked up some. "I'm good." I squeezed my fingers, drawnin' our contact closer, then leaned in his direction, seekin' the comfort of bein' at his side.

"You down with spendin' a day or two here?"

My eyes widened. No doubt I'd been spacin' when they'd been makin' plans. He must have read alarm rather than surprise in my eyes, because his entire body reacted. He stopped walkin' and turned me into him so we were standin' face-to-face.

A dimple danced on his cheek, and he licked his lips before he spoke. "We can swoop up Kayla and bounce if you feel better 'bout that."

I heard him, but couldn't reply. I was straight up too busy starin' at his lips, left shiny and wet from where his tongue had been, all swarmed into the memory of those lips on me.

His dimples deepened, as he musta known what I was thinkin' 'cause he kissed me right quick. Not long or deep. Lawdy, just a little peck, but enough for me to know I wanted more.

When he lifted his head his dark eyes were shimmering with a smile. He stroked his thumb across my palm. "Anythang you want, shortie."

What I wanted was another kiss. Another night in the hotel room. Another chance to go all the way. Another chance to show him I cared enough to be his girl.

To spend more time with him.

"We'll stay."

He grinned, then his gaze roamed over to James and Kayla, who were watchin' us, but pretendin' they weren't. "Fo' sheedo? I want ya to be sure."

"Yeah, Maurice. I like marinatin' with ya. We'll stay." Then I kissed him again, fast and shallow, like he kissed me a sec ago, 'cause I couldn't help it. And I didn't give a damn 'bout Kayla's giggles or knowin' looks.

I wanted Maurice as my man. Time to fess up publicly. Or at least to my cousin. My face flushed. I winked at her as I turned away from Maurice. "Let's eat." I touched my free hand to my stomach. "I'm dyin'."

CHAPTER 19

I **hella** wanted to talk to Kayla alone, but the rest of the afternoon we never really got the chance. After walkin' across campus, James found us this little burger joint where I wolfed down food hexa fast, but said little.

James and Maurice did most the talkin', sprinklin' facts 'bout the hoods they'd each grown up in, 'bout sports they played, 'bout clean rides and fly gold rims.

And it'd been sorta funny, too, like two couples who'd known each other forever, when really James was the newcomer to the crew. But you wouldn't know it by the way he laughed and exchanged, and if anythin' I was the one on the outs, kinda quiet as I watched my cousin *oooh* and *aaaah* over this boy.

Though he seemed aiight, I still couldn't shake the feelin' that Kayla had moved too fast with him, and there was gonna be drama when it was time to pull up and go home. All through dinner I kept my lips and questions in check, knowin' I was hella quizzin' her when I got her alone.

Maurice musta noticed my lack of participation in the conversation because more than once he'd stroke his thumb across my palm and give my hand a little reassuring squeeze. When his dark, rich gaze met mine, I could hella feel how much he understood 'bout me.

And I loved him for it. Knots tightened up in my belly. I loved this boy, in this deep, intense way I'd never felt before. I repressed a tremor right quick and just tried to enjoy bein' there with him.

And I waited to get K alone. I needed to talk to her in this unexplainable crazy-ass way. We'd always shared so much—well, except my GettinHooked motives and my feelings for her neighbor—and I kinda feared right 'bout now she was keepin' big-time secrets from me.

But we never really got the chance to talk in private. By the time we'd finished eatin', the desert sun had started to fade all quick-like, and the warm air split, too, leavin' me chilled.

It was a different kinda cold than The Bay, dry but nipping, and before I knew what was down, Maurice had me tucked all cozy against his warm, solid side, with an arm wrapped snug around my back. I could hella dig the way his hand felt restin' on my hip, the way his fingers crept beneath my shirt to sweep along my skin.

And here and there he offered up the cutest little looks that had his amazing dark eyes sparklin' and his dimples cuttin' holes in his cheeks.

Since the sun had set, James skipped showin' us more of the 'Zona State campus, and we headed back to his dorm instead. He'd already told Maurice and me that we could crash there tonight, if we wanted to share his roommate's single bed. His roommate had gone home for spring break, so the room was his for the next week.

And during the walk back to Irish Hall, James had suggested going to this club he knew 'bout where his fella bounced the door.

"I don't have a license," I'd said, straight-up worried 'bout going clubbin' where I didn't know any of the peeps. Though, I had to admit, there was something exciting and grown 'bout it, too.

"Just show him some sort of ID so his boss thinks he's checkin' but we're in regardless." James laughed and nodded a "you know" at Maurice.

Kayla was all excited 'bout it, her wide blue eyes pleading with me to go along. She even did this little hair flip, titling her head to the side like she used to do when we were little and she wanted me to do somethin' for her.

I glanced slowly at Maurice. He dark gaze was gentle and understandin', like he'd be chill with whatever I decided. His hand rested on my hip, his fingers strokin' all soft-like against my skin beneath my shirt, and right quick my mind flashed to what we'd be doin' tonight if we didn't go clubbin'.

And all of a sudden clubbin' felt less dangerous. Less adventurous. And fa sheezy, less thrillin', 'cause if we were just gonna kick it, me and Maurice, I kinda knew in that moment we'd be gettin' down to business.

"Whatever you wanna do, shortie." Maurice's voice was low, just meant for me and soothed and stirred like crazy. He lowered his voice, lickin' his lips in the hella sexxi way. "Whatever you want."

It straight up wasn't easy, but I tugged my eyes from his and looked back at Kayla and James, standing just a few feet away still holdin' hands.

"Aiight, we'll go."

I heard Maurice's little disappointed breath, and I knew he must have been thinkin' the same thang I'd been.

"Yay, girl, you won't be sorry," Kayla said, breakin' free of James to give me a quick little hug.

"I didn't really bring nothing to wear. Just sweats."

"I packed tons of clean gear, Imani." She was back by James's side and we were walkin' again, toward his dorm. "We'll find you somethin' hexa cute."

It didn't take long before we were back where he stayed, the dorm tucked all up in Irish Hall. And just a few minutes later Kayla and I were grabbin' up towels, headed toward the community showers.

It was kinda weird at first, thinking 'bout sharing a bathroom with a bunch of strangers, but actually it was more private than the showers we took after PE back at Howard.

Each shower had its own stall and shower curtain, and Kayla had told me that the hot water lasted forever, since the dorms were close to deserted because so many had skipped out for spring break.

I'd been hopin' that it would end up bein' just me and my cousin in the shared bathrooms, that we'd finally get the chance to talk a little. Time to confess how I felt about Maurice—how deep it really was—and time for me to find out exactly what had gone down between my cousin and her man.

But we weren't alone. There were a few other girls, all apparently getting ready to go out, too, and so they showered a few stalls down, with their curtains closed, but they talked and laughed, while I pretty much kept my quiet.

I kinda felt weird, and hella outta place, a junior in high school with these girls who were in college, even if they didn't look a whole lot older, and by the way they were acting and giggling, they didn't seem a whole older, either.

I didn't have time to do my hair the way I wanted, 'cause pressing it straight would take hella long and I knew the boys would be waiting. So I tossed some curl definer in there instead and hoped that my wild curls wouldn't frizz too bad since we were away from the dampness of The Bay.

I shaved my legs in the shower, then smoothed them with some sweet-smellin' lotion from Bath & Body Works so they'd look hella tight for the tiny Baby Phat mini Kayla had found for me to borrow. I rubbed the same lotion across my lower stomach, left bare by the small halter top, and across my shoulders, too.

I was damn near naked; it was all gravy though, because just the thought of Maurice seeing me like this left me feelin' hella warm inside.

Kayla was wearin' just as few clothes, and just as she pulled on her skirt, I caught sight of the small purple marks dottin' low on her hip and below her belly button. I knew what I was peepin'. Hickies.

My throat felt all tight as I pulled my gaze away from the love bites, wantin' bad to ask her 'bout them, but knowin' we couldn't have this discussion in front of the other girls that were in the bathroom gettin' fly.

So just like before, I bit the inside of my cheek as we quit the bathroom and headed back to James's room. He'd stuck a shoe between the jam and the door to hold it open just a little for us to come back in without knockin'.

Maurice was sittin' on the bed that'd be ours for the night, lacing up his Jordans. He glanced up as soon as we came in, his eyes lockin' right on me, his smile small and a little tight. But even as his smile looked somewhat skeptical, I could read the appreciation dancing in the twinkle of his midnight stare.

"You look gooood." If he'd said the words aloud, I hadn't heard it, I just saw the way his full lips moved and knew I wanted him to kiss me again, the way he had this mornin' in the bed.

His gaze was so strong that I hella forgot 'bout everythang else in the room. Kayla and James were talkin' but I didn't hear a single word, just the mumbled tones of their voices.

"Thanks," I whispered.

He stood up, lifting his jacket from the bed next to him as he walked my way. He'd changed, too, I noticed for the first time, into some dark blue baggie jeans and a button shirt over a white tee.

"It's gonna be cold," he said, putting his Bape across my shoulders.

It smelled so hexa good, like washing powder and his cologne. I squeezed my lids closed right quick and inhaled as I surrounded myself in the warmth of his jacket, and I heard his low chuckle rumble low and rich at the back of his throat.

I knew it was goin' to be cold outside, but that wasn't

the reason he'd given me his Bape. I knew why. *To cover me up.* I felt like laughin' but kept my chill, because fo' sheezy, I dug it. With the clothes Kayla had lent me, I was more naked than dressed and headed out in public.

And oh, lawdy, I hecka liked the little bit of protective possessiveness puttin' his jacket over me proved.

"You two ready?" James moved toward us, interrupting our moment of peepin' and appreciatin'.

"Yup, let's bounce." Maurice opened the door, then held it open for me. As soon as we were in the hallway, his hand caught mine up and he linked our fingers.

Kayla's itty-bitty bit of clothing was covered by an oversize black ASU hoodie and, of course, James was hugged up close beside her as we ditched his buildin' walkin' back into the cool night air.

"You go here a lot?" Kayla asked, after we'd walked a few minutes.

"Yeah, I guess. Weekends mostly."

"It's fun?" It was the first time I'd heard the hitch of hesitation in Kayla's voice. I know it sounds whack, but her slight nervousness actually helped ease mine. I thought I was hella trippin' to be unsure, but since I wasn't the only one it eased me off a little.

"Yeah, it's good. You can meet some of my peeps."

"Your boys hoop?" Maurice asked, turnin' the conversation back to sports, stats and free throws.

So we walked across the campus, over this tight-ass bridge that led over the street and past the fields, then off campus. We weren't alone in the briskness of the clear night. Groups of people roamed 'bout, headed one place or another.

Sometimes James would offer up a quick greetin', and sometimes we just walked on by. It was kinda weird to see so many folks out, 'cause not even when there was a party going down back home did we ever just see people hangin' outside like we did tonight. Not in our hood.

And then we were there. I heard the beats and bumps before I saw the gathering crowds or the lights. But the *thump-a-thump* of my pulse raged in time and it was enough to know we were gonna have a crazy-ass wild night.

CHAPTER 20

I'm not sure what I'd been expecting, but hell nah, it wasn't this. After waiting in line with a couple dozen other folks, we were finally let inside the club. Gettin' in went down just like James said it would. At the door we showed our IDs: Maurice his Cali driver's license, Kayla and I our high school cards.

James's boy peeped 'em out, then glanced at our faces, then let us through like he'd made sure were old enough to be inside a club that served alcohol.

I'd been to plenty of kickbacks and pallays, I knew the music would be loud and folks would be actin' a fool. But I hadn't anticipated the low lights throughout; the only brightness was the brilliant neon slung up to backlight a row of booze behind a long bar.

Standing on my tippy-toes and grippin' Maurice's hand, I glanced 'bout, tryin' to see over the tops of heads. A system had been set up in the back corner on a small stage and there was a dude workin' the table hella hard, spinnin' track after track and mixin' them up.

The bump of bass vibrated along my skin, the *boom-boom* findin' its place in my blood. Not exactly dancing, I moved with the beats, a roll of the head, a rotation of the shoulders. And the crowd moved in time, too, shiftin' and swayin' as one song scratched into the next.

Toward the center of the dance floor there was a few boys krumpin' wild-like, hittin' it and doing a battle. Kids at home had done this, too, but here, mixed with the flow of drinks and hyped sounds, each hard stomp, each wiggle and shuffle, seemed way more intense.

"I'll get us something to drink," James shouted to be heard over the tunes.

I could see Maurice nod, but I didn't say crap, too focused on takin' in all my surroundings, the movements, the tiny-ass pieces of clothing, the grillz, the frillz, all the feet covered with Jordans.

I'm not sure how long James was gone, but it only felt like a quick sec before he was back with drinks.

"Here." He handed out glasses.

Accepting without really looking, I brought it to my lips and drank it, then screwed up my face at the bitterness. "It's beer."

"Yup."

I'd had drinks before, but never did dig the taste. Glancin' at my cousin, I could tell she didn't really like it, either, even though she was fo' shizzle sippin'.

Stretchin' out my hand, I went to hand the glass back to James. "You drink it, I don't really like it."

"You don't like to drink?"

Hell nah, I didn't. It made folks act hella stupid even though there was something a little fun about the goofy feelin' a few drinks created.

Chill, girl, this little inner voice murmured. I was away from home. Slantin' my gaze from Kayla to Maurice, I hexa knew I just wanted this to be a good time, forget about consequences.

"I just don't like the way beer tastes."

"So you want something else?"

"Sure." I shrugged. Just for a moment I wondered if this was 'bout tryin' to fit in. Takin' a deep breath, then exhaling all slow-like, I let go of it…let it slide away. Nothin' wrong with having a little fun.

The song changed, the chant makin' me want to move my feet, to shake-shake my thang. Unlacing my fingers from Maurice's, I stepped away from him, joining the folks bumpin' the floor.

By the time song ended, my heart rate had stepped it up and my body was warm. When I looked back to where I'd left them standing, I realized James had returned and was holding a small glass filled with something blue.

And Maurice was still standin' there, too, the smile in his eyes shimmering as he watched me. I smiled back, then moved in their direction, acceptin' the drink from James as I approached.

"What is it?"

"Good." He grinned wide, his now free hand reaching for Kayla's.

"Oh..." I took a sip. *Good* was right. The cool blue fluid was sweet and slightly fruity. Though I could still taste the nasty of alcohol, it was faint compared to anything else I'd tasted.

"You like it?" Kayla asked.

"Yup." I drank deeper, the swallow feelin' hella good on my throat after dancing.

She turned toward James. "Can you get me one?"

"Me, too." I handed him back my empty cup, then grinned all sassy-like at Maurice, who chuckled low in this throat beside me. Liftin' on my tippy-toes, I whispered in his ear, "It's good." As I moved away, I intentionally brushed my lips across his skin, just enough to hear him catch his breath right quick.

And then I was struttin' away from him, smilin' as I shimmied back toward the edge of the dance floor, where I was welcomed into the mix of bumpers 'n grinders. Girls were laughin' around me, their arms in the air, their hips swivelin'. And there were fellas there, too, movin' in time with the *thump-thump-thump* of the beat.

By the time the song—or two, I'm not sure, 'cause I lost track—ended I was feelin' as warm inside as I was dampened by sweat formin' on my skin. I wasn't faded, but fa sheezy, I could feel the effects of the booze.

Cool fingers linked with mine, drawin' my attention as I danced, too small and delicate to be Maurice's. Lookin' back, all I saw was long strands of blond hair bouncin' over Kayla's face.

She angled toward me, lifting her voice to be heard, "Oh, my gawd, girl. This is hella tight."

I nodded. The club was off the chain.

I'm not sure when it happened. I was havin' a hexa hard time keepin' track of time, keepin' track of which song blended into the next, *shit,* thinkin' clear at all. Things moved fast around me, bodies shifting, arms, people seeping like water. But things were moving slow, too. Colors blurred, patterns stopped makin' sense.

I was just groovin', the rhythm taking up residence in my body. Just dancing, and then he was there. Maurice was behind me, his hand on my waist, his hips grindin' into me. Laughin', I turned in his arms, grabbin' hold of his shirt, drawing him closer.

He laughed, too, his body tremblin' beneath my touch as my hands found their way beneath his shirt to smooth across soft skin and hard muscle. It's not easy to remember, but I think we were in the middle of the floor, bass blaring heavy around us, bodies brushin' against us, dancin' like everyone else was.

But it felt like we were alone. Just Maurice and me. Just his large frame. Just his hands. Just his lips. As the club faded away, the crowds, the noise, all I could see or feel was him. And I wanted to kiss him. I wanted to be with him. Really be with him.

I wanted, now more than ever—almost desperately—to be his girl.

"Kiss me."

Had I said that aloud? I wasn't sure, but before the thought, or the words, were clear his mouth was on mine. It was sweet at first, just a brushin' of lips, just a slow glide of tongue. Then the kiss deepened. And we stopped dancin' and just stood there makin' out.

His hands roamed all free-like across my back, skimmed lightly over my waist, arced over my butt until he gripped the backs of my thighs and pulled me closer. I think I made some little moanie noise because he found a way to angle his head and stroke his tongue between my teeth.

And I gripped his shirt at his sides, holding on tight so the world wouldn't spin away from me. So I wouldn't fall into a puddle of goo at his feet. So my bones wouldn't melt leavin' me unable to stand without his help.

I was standin' in a club in Arizona with Maurice

makin' out. I laughed against his mouth. I couldn't help it, it just seemed so hella silly to me.

The kiss ended. Maurice chuckled, too, and let me loose a little. But before I stepped too far back, he was draggin' me back into his embrace and huggin' me hella tight.

Things were a little hazy now, but it didn't seem like he hugged me long before he was whisperin' in my ear, "Walk it out, girl," and movin' back to do the moves of the song. I laughed and joined him, shufflin' my feet, pumpin' my arms in rhythm with the rhymes.

It was all gravity, baby, as I danced a few steps away from Maurice and turned, tryin' hecka hard to focus on finding where Kayla and James where dancing.

I could see them a few couples over bumpin' and grindin' and doing their thang. Kayla looked over just then, and I returned her wide smile as she ground into her man.

A large hand settled on my upper arm, givin' me a little tug. Thinkin' it was Maurice, I turned into him ready for more of those yum-yum kisses and gentle caresses. Only it wasn't Maurice, but some other dude.

"Hey, tender, lemme get atcha."

I pulled my arm away. Or tried to. His hold was firm. "Let me go."

"Come on. You're bangin', girl. Holla atcha ya boy, I know you been lookin' for me."

It was hard to focus. I squeezed my lids closed, then opened them again but it did little good. He wasn't going to let my arm go, so I scanned behind him lookin' for Maurice.

I have a man, I wanted to shout at him, but with my mind buzzin' hard I was hella worried he'd know I was lying. "You're trippin'. I'm not lookin' for you or any guy." Maurice was the only one I wanted.

"Yeah, right."

"Lemme go! I'm not lookin' for anyone." I was shoutin' now, because my heart was pounding against my ribs and it was gettin' hard to breathe, or because the music was so loud it was the only way to be heard.

"I saw your profile. I know you need what I got for ya." He grabbed his crotch with his free hand.

"You're talkin' 'bout my shortie." It was Maurice's voice, coming from directly behind me. Lawdy, just in time.

"This beezy ain't yours." The dude's fingers were tightening painfully on my upper arm.

Maurice shoved the dude hella hard in the chest. "Call her a bitch again." It was a taunt, a dare.

Because the guy was grippin' me, I stumbled back as he did, but was kept from fallin' as Maurice stepped in my direction and put his arm around my waist. Maybe 'cause he was off balance, or maybe 'cause he knew he was no match for Maurice, the guy's hand slipped from my arm.

Immediately Maurice was steppin' forward, puttin' himself between me 'n the other boy. His hands were fisted by his sides, his chest forward, chin high.

"Why ya blockin', brah?"

"Step off, punk, she got a man."

I did? "No, I don't." Snap, did I say that aloud, too? Both of their gazes shifted to me.

The other guy scoffed. Maurice's dark gaze locked on mine for a sec, and I swear, there was somethin' jealous and possessive there.

The other dude laughed. "See, she jeepin' you." He grabbed his crotch again. "Maybe you not puttin' on your twirk good 'nuff."

And with one thump, the dude hit the floor, Maurice lettin' his fist rain.

I narrowed my eyes, tryin' to get rid of the blur, tryin' hella hard to get rid of the feelin' of being a little unsteady.

My heart was poundin', my pulse racing. I couldn't think straight. Biting my lips so I wouldn't scream, I watched the scene unravel.

The guy had called me a slut and Maurice was fightin' him. Beatin' the shit out of him.

And then other fellas poured into the mix, some fists flyin' but most tryin' to pull Maurice off and hold him back. A couple other guys were fightin' now, their hands flyin' up.

James was there then, both his hands on Maurice's shoulders as he shoved him back. "Take Imani outside," he ordered, tryin' to get a handle on what was goin' down. "I've got this." He angled his heard toward the door. "Bounce, dawg."

Maurice nodded, turnin' toward me, but I was already moving away, trying to shove past people to get to the exit. I stumbled a couple times, my entire body tremblin', my knees feelin' like they were about to give way.

I could feel Maurice on my heels, feel the heat of him as his palm settled on the small of my back and urged me along.

We were through the doors now, and being splashed with the cool night air. It felt good rushin' across my cheeks, across my body that was mostly exposed. My skin bare.

My step faltered, but Maurice didn't slow. "Over there." And he angled us so that we entered the shadows around the corner of the buildin', hidden from the glow of the streetlights.

"Why'd you say that?"

Huh? I closed my eyes, tryin' hexa hard to recall what I'd said that he could question, but my mind couldn't wrap around the memory, shiftin' from one event to the next. Circling back again.

"What?"

"That you don't have a man." There was emotion in his low, rough tone that I couldn't read, anger or pain, I wasn't sure.

I swallowed. "I don't," I whispered, my cheeks going all warm. I slanted my gaze away.

His fingertips touched my cheek, slowly brushin' back my wild curls. The slight caress was so tender it kinda shocked me that it was by the same hand that had just put the busta on the floor.

"Imani." His voice was soft, just above a whisper as he turned my face back to his. "What am I to you, then?"

I shrugged. We'd been hangin' out for weeks and yet I'd never told him how I felt. Never told him what I wanted from him. I'd had plenty of opportunities. But I hadn't.

I hadn't been halfway to faded before, either. Now the words just spilled out. "I want you to be, Maurice, but you never asked. Never said a word about being my boo."

"Shortie, I'm your boo." He smiled. I wanted to see his dimples, but I could only tell he was grinning by the brightness of his teeth in the dim evening light.

"You are?"

"Yeah, 'n' I know I never asked you, but I'm askin' you now. Will you be my girl?"

I held my breath right quick, too afraid that if I

breathed wrong maybe I'd wake up in my bed in The Bay. Plus, my head was a little fuzzed and I didn't want to ever forget this.

He was askin' me. This thang happened inside me. Just a few little words and I belonged. Warmth traveled along my skin and I hella wanted to giggle.

Instead I grabbed his shirt, tightenin' my hands around the material and dragged him closer. "I'm your girl." And then I kissed him, liftin' on my toes again. Kissed him firm, pressing my lips to his.

But I kept it short, broken up by the bubblin' up of my laughter. Using my hands still curled around his clothes, I thrust him away from me. "Now, go get my cousin out of there so we can pixx out."

He was chucklin' as he turned away. "Anythang for my girl."

CHAPTER 21

PACIN' the sidewalk a little, I waited for Maurice to come back, bringing Kayla and James with him. People mingled around me, some comin', some goin', but most were laughing and having a good time.

And no one really noticed me as I moved back and forth, tryin' to find my balance as the drinks and recent events swayed through me.

I straight up admit it: I'd been a little more than buzzed off two small drinks. I still have no idea what they were, except hella yummy-tastin'. But I've only had drinks a few times before, so I guess I wasn't really a heavy.

Still, as the cool night air washed across my skin, things were shapin' up in my brain, clearin' out. Or maybe the fuzz-a-fuzz started walkin' when Maurice turned my crush into a couple. Us.

I turned on my heel, spinnin' back toward the club,

the music pulsin' into the darkness. Deep breaths, deep breaths are what I needed so things would stop spinnin'. So things would be steady and I could think clearly.

In through my nose, I exhaled past parted lips. I couldn't quit trippin' on the irony of how thangs had played out. Yet there was so much to still patch up.

Mostly facin' up to the dangers of Gettin-Hooked.com. Time to figure out a way to convince Kayla what a bad idea it was without gettin' into another argument. Without makin' myself stand out like a spoiled brat, since I already had exactly what I wanted.

Maurice. And there he was walkin' toward me, just to the left of Kayla and James. But *she* did have James.

My cousin broke away from the guys and ran my way, huggin' me close when she got here. "Oh, my gawd, Imani, wasn't that off the hook?"

I laughed. "Fa shizzle. Everythang except for the fight." I glanced at Maurice, but they were still a few yards away.

Kayla wrapped her hand around mine. "Come on." She skipped in her heels, tugging me along with her, tipsy, laughin' and swingin' our arms between us like we had when we were little.

The few yards got a little deeper, but I could tell the boys were still trailin' after us. And talkin'.

Here we were, on the streets of 'Zona, and finally alone. Finally able to talk for a sec. As our spirited feet began to slow, and our pace chilled out, I glanced at Kayla, her eyes dancin' in the darkness, her pale hair glittering under the street lighting.

"Why'd he knock that dude?"

Huh? My thoughts wondered, and I hadn't realized we were talkin' about what had happened in the club. "Oh, he called me a bitch."

"For realz?" My cousin paused, turnin' toward me. "So Maurice did the pow-wow." She demonstrated with a punch in the air.

I giggled, only halfway sobered up. "Yup. He couldn't just let the scrub talk 'bout *his girl*."

"His girl?" She squealed, clappin' her hands together all cheerleader-like. "I knew. Snap, you shoulda told me."

I shrugged. "I guess." Yeah, I shoulda told her, because then we wouldn't be this far from home. We wouldn't be facin' all our friends bein' hella pissed when we closed down the site they were all crazy-diggin'.

I inhaled sharply, then let the air whistle through my teeth, gettin' set for the next part. "K, Maurice hit that guy 'cause of Gettin' Hooked."

"Whattayamean?"

"He saw me online. Saw my profile, and knew I

was lookin' to be hooked with a guy. He thought it should be him."

"Maurice had other ideas." She glanced over her shoulder back at the fellas, who seemed to have slowed. Maybe to give us a few moments of privacy. "You two are so, so cute together."

Yeah, like there was any way I coulda not grin. I felt the smile spread like sunshine through me. I lifted a shoulder and slanted my head, that goofy love-struck look I'd seen on others was now fo' sho' plastered on my face. "I guess."

She laughed.

"Kayla."

"Yeah, girl."

"We gotta shut it down."

There was silence for a sec. We strolled on, our hands still entwined like kindergarteners, like the friends we'd been all of our lives. Like the bond of blood we shared could ever be weakened.

"How come?" she finally said, but her tone held very little conviction.

"It's dangerous."

"It's not. James is cool, ya know that."

I nodded. "You got lucky. He coulda been a rapist or killer."

Again the silence seeped through the night around us, just the *click-click* of our heels poppin' off on the pavement and a few distant chuckles from the guys strollin' yards behind us.

"It's dangerous, Kayla. We're in Arizona. No tellin' what happens to the next girl who finds a non-local boy and goes after him like you did. One of our friends."

Her shoulders heaved and I heard the whisper of her sighin' breath.

I tightened my fingers around her hand, offerin' the same sort of reassurance Maurice had served me up with the last couple of days. "You understand, right? We gotta shut it down."

"Aiight, I guess we need to." My cousin looked back again, the winked at me. "Besides, did you peep what I've got?"

Laughter eased the hella coiled tension. "Yup, yup. He's cute."

Quiet again, but I knew my cousin well and she was thinkin', tryin' to decide how much to tell me before I even asked her 'bout what had gone down between the two of 'em.

"We went all the way." Her voice was low and sweet, and so purely innocent it was whack mixed with what she was tellin' me.

"I know."

"You do?"

I bit my lip and nodded. "You okay?"

Kayla laughed. "Yeah, it was hexa niiice."

Hexa niiice…and I knew that's all she was gonna say 'bout it tonight. So though I wanted to know more, I let it go. Let the questions slide away. For now.

We'd strolled to the end of the block where we'd have to head over the bridge back onto campus, so we paused to wait for our boys. The building was wrapped in black plate-glass windows that were actin' like mirrors in the dark.

Feelin' our bodies sway gently in shoes that were too high for two teen girls who couldn't hold their liquor, we hugged to hold each other steady. We laughed, then sighed, our hands still gripped.

Turnin' together, we tipped our heads together so my wild brown curls tangled with her smooth blonde strands, our faces smilin' and starin' back at us.

Lifting my free hand, I traced the shape of my almond eyes in the cool glass, then did the same to my cousin's. She smiled, the contrast of her blue eyes was so different than mine, but the shape was the same.

Then I traced the fullness of my lips, the black-girl in me.

"We look alike," I whispered. We always had. The shape of our faces, the angles along our jaws, the small bridge of the noses. Since our coloring was so different, sometimes I forgot all 'bout what made us the same.

"Fo' sho', we look the same, we're cousins." She

raised her free hand and traced the reflection of our eyes just as I had done. "We have my mom's eyes."

Oh, lawdy, there it was, her mom, sister to mine. "And mine, too, I guess."

"Yeah, you look like her."

My heart skipped a beat, then seized. The breath that'd been in my lungs now burned and the sting of tears threatened at the back of my eyes. "Do you see her?" The words were forced through my dry and closin' throat. "Do you see my momma?"

It was the drinks. It was the emotion of pent-up years of wondering. It was learning Kayla wasn't a virgin. Of being Maurice's girl.

It was everythang.

We were seventeen and I'd never asked my cousin if she saw her auntie, like I saw mine all the damn time. I think maybe 'cause the answer could devastate me, because there was more of me than not that hella didn't wanna know.

But she told me anyway. "Yes."

Just the one little word. Just three little letters. *And everything changed.*

In the reflecting glass I saw my eyes fill with tears, so I lowered my eyes and squeezed them closed. I'd grown up makin' up excuses for her absence—like maybe she was dead—tryin' to come up with reasons why she wouldn't wanna mom me.

The color of my skin always spinnin' back to me. The kinkiness of my hair. The wideness of my nose. Brown eyes, unlike her blue.

My lip trembled, so I tucked it between my teeth. I heard the male voices coming closer, I wanted them there so we couldn't talk 'bout this no more. I wanted them to stay away so I could know everything. And I wanted the buzz of being halfway-to-faded to go away so I could think. There were questions, so many fuckin' questions I needed answers to.

But Kayla spoke before I could put voice to the shattered dreams of girlhood.

"Not very often, Imani. Just twice a year."

"Where is she?" I sounded like a frickin' toad.

"San Diego."

I opened my eyes, the tears leakin' down my cheeks now. My voice broke. "How come she didn't want me?"

My cousin stood there motionless. Her blue gaze filled with sorrow and sympathy and compassion, but unable to supply what I needed right 'bout then.

The truth.

"I don't think it was you, Imani." She touched my shoulder. "It wasn't you. She just didn't want to be a mom anymore."

"After a year? I was just a year when she left me!" I was losing control. "She shoulda thought about that shit before she spread her legs." It's what Gram had said. She just said it nicer.

I swallowed, tryin' to chill, tryin' to slow the rapid fire of my heart rate. "Does she ask about me?"

Kayla was cryin' now, too. Silver droplets slithered down her peaches-and-cream skin. "No." It was just above a whisper. "But your Gram sends her pictures sometimes and—"

"Gram! Gram knows 'bout this?" And then things hella started clickin' into place. All the bitterness Gram had, even after all these damn years. All along she'd been reachin' out to my mother, tryin' to make her part of my life. The pictures on my gram's lap flashed right quick through my memory.

The pictures she'd hidden from me. Just like the honesty I needed. All my life everyone had lied while smilin' pretty in my face and tellin' me they loved me.

I yanked my hand away from Kayla's, betrayal cuttin' deep, stealin' the last screwed-up shreds of my control. I stepped back. Away from her. My knees wobbled, but I steadied myself. All by myself. Alone, like I'd always been. Oh, I know my daddy loved me, but he was gone more than home. And I know Gram had done what she could, but all the goodness was dashed away by what she never gave.

The information I needed.

"I'm the only one who doesn't know?"

She nodded.

"It's my momma," I screamed, the words chokin' me, the tears flowin' hexa fast now. "And no one told me shit!"

Confused and hurt, hurtin' so bad I thought I might die of it, I turned and fled. Ran into the night, caressed by the privacy of darkness.

I could hear my sobs, hear the clickin' of my shoes, hear my heart breakin'.

And I could hear the heavy falls of Maurice's feet as he chased after me. Maurice came. The only one I could count on.

CHAPTER 22

kayla and James had had sex again. I knew from the first sec I walked back into James's dorm room. The room was dark, aside from the green digital clock and the glowin' yellow of the low-playin' stereo.

The heat felt heavy, especially compared to the crispness of the nighttime outdoors. And it smelled of sweat and booty-juice like it does at house parties when folks have shaken their asses a little too hard.

My eyes slowly adjustin' to the darkness, I stood just inside the entryway of the room, Maurice's big body warm and solid right behind me. No damn way did I wanna catch them in the act, so I closed my eyes and listened for movements or signs of action comin' from the bed.

When I heard nada, I narrowed my eyes as my gaze traveled to the narrow bed they shared, ready to slam my lids shut again if they were smashin'. The covers were wrapped around them and both were asleep. The slow, long breaths gave them away.

They both had shirts on, but I was hella sure that was for our benefit. Kayla's blond hair was a ratty mess, one bare leg dangled out of under the blankets. I stared at her, tryin' hella hard to repress the resentment I felt. The anger over the secrets she'd kept from me.

Me. Her best friend. Her cousin. Her blood.

Though I tried to bottle it up, a shiver traveled down my spine. I think maybe my brain was tryin' to sort out the mess of all the straight-up junk that happened to me tonight.

Or maybe it was just my body gettin' used to the heat of the room, slowly startin' to shed the chill. Or it coulda been the faint odor of what they'd done earlier that was trippin' me out.

At least they'd lit a stick of incense, the rose scent leavin' the odor of sex faint. But still there. My stomach hurt and I had to swallow down my gag reflex.

My gaze roamed slowly to the bed I'd be sharin' with Maurice tonight. It was half the size of the one we'd shared the night before, and even with all that space we'd come close doin' the do.

Tonight we'd be pressed closer. But we'd also be sharin' a room. I gulped a breath of air. I was so confused, wantin' to share myself with my boy, wantin' him to be my first. I'd wanted that for a long time.

But I'd be a liar if I said I wasn't scared. My knees wobbled with it. I knew it wouldn't go down tonight, not with Kayla and James a bed away. Wouldn't be special here, like it's supposed to be. But it would happen with us. It was the *one* thing I was sure 'bout tonight. Him.

He must have guessed at what I was thinkin', hangin' back by the door, my head angled toward the bed we'd be gettin' in.

His hand touched my shoulder, now covered in his blue Bape jacket. Gentle, but so reassuring, he held me, then leaned forward to whisper in my ear. "I'll just hold ya tonight."

Like he'd held me for the last couple hours.

With no place to go after Maurice caught up with me, we'd found a bench tucked away along an unlit walkway on campus. And then Maurice had held me on his lap, his jacket thrown over us, his strong arms holdin' me tight as my body shook with sobs.

He kept on holdin' me, too, with one hand strokin', sensitive-like, up and down my spine. And he listened as I poured out all the pain of the knife wedged into my heart. Then he'd murmur just the right thangs, tenderly wiping away my tears.

So we'd sat that way for hours, warm in each other's arms, but in the cold of deep night. Just me and him, nearly a thousand miles from home, in a cocoon of darkness and understandin'.

"Hold me, then." It was just a whisper, just a mere mouthin' of the words as I glanced over my shoulder at him, his profile so hexa fine in the shadows. Twinin' our fingers so he fell into step with me when I moved toward the bed, I wanted him to know how much I dug what he'd done for me on this whack-ass night.

"Hold me, boo."

He chuckled low in his throat, then kicked off his shoes. I dropped his jacket over the back of a chair. Though I'd brought something to sleep in, I didn't wanna make a fuss over lookin' for it. I'd sleep in the small mini and halter top. Heck, it was almost like bein' nothin' but bra and panties.

"Do you want the wall?" he asked, his voice low and close.

"No." I pressed a hand to my stomach. It'd been rollin' and a tad unsettled since the fog of alcohol wore off. "In case I need the bathroom."

His laugh broke through the stillness. "I'm feelin' ya."

He settled into the bed, his back to the wall. We'd have had more room if I'd put my back to his chest, spoon style, but I wanted to look at him. Wanted to be able to see the glimmer in his eyes, the cuteness of his dimples, lips that made me weak. So I got in facin' him, then drew the blanket up over us.

His arm wrapped around me, the cool night lingerin'

on his skin and clothing, he cuddled me all tender like. It'd be dawn in a few hours. We'd be leavin' in the mornin'. I knew that and I was ready. Ready to go home and face the mess of thangs left behind there. Ready to deal with my daddy and Gram. Ready to confront the anger of my friends when Gettin-Hooked.com was shut down.

But tonight? I just wasn't ready to let it end.

"Maurice?"

His eyes were closed, I could see his lashes restin' on his cheeks. "Hmm."

Squeezin' an arm between us, I touched his face. Like I'd done my eyes in the window, I traced the shape of his lips with my fingertips. But he was warm and hella real. My image had been an illusion.

His breath caressed my hand as he smiled.

"I've liked ya forevah." His smile widened, I could feel it in the darkness. My fingers moved from his lips to smooth across the dents of his dimples. The booze was long gone, so there was no blamin' it for my confessin'. Just showin' my boo my heart, he'd seen so much of it tonight already.

"Ya have?"

"Fa shizzle."

He shifted. His hand came up and brushed aside a few outta-control curls, then stroked his palm across my hair. "How come ya never said nothin' 'bout likin' me?"

"I wanted to."

"You shoulda."

There was a lump in my throat that I had to swallow twice to get rid of. "I was afraid." The whisper was so low I wasn't sure he heard me at first. He was silent, his breath even. Maybe he'd fallen asleep.

I allowed my fingers to slide across his skin, now losin' the feel of bein' outside. Through the murkiness of darkness, I stared at his mouth, the smile slightly faded now, his lips full and temptin'. Figurin' he'd fallen asleep, I resisted the urge to kiss him as I wanted to.

"Afraid of what?"

His hoarse drowsy words startled me. Liftin' my gaze to his eyes, I realized he wasn't sleepin' but starin' straight at me, all intense and unwaverin'.

"That..." I cleared my throat. "That you didn't like me, too."

"We been marinatin' for a minute, shortie." His thumb stroked across my cheek and he brushed aside my hair again. He kissed me, light and unexpected, on my lips.

"Lots of peeps hang out."

"Cup cakin', that's what I been doin' with ya."

When we'd come back here tonight, I'd hella thought I'd cried out all my crazy-ass tears. I was wrong. They burned in my eyes now and seeped from my lashes.

"Don't do that, Imani." A tear landed on his fingers.

"Don't cry over me, girl. Don't ever cry over me. I promise, I'll never give ya reason."

Oh, lawdy, I was hexa losin' it tonight, makin' a straight fool of myself. I sniffled, figuring that wasn't much after all the boo-hooing I'd done earlier on his shoulder. "Oh." *Dayum,* could that have sounded any more pathetic?

"I've been feelin' ya, too, for a long-ass time."

My heart did this little rat-a-tat beat hard against my ribs, makin' me wonder if Maurice could feel it, we were that close. My pulse was hella pickin' up speed. "Why didn't you say anything?"

"Was 'bout to ask Kayla if you were talkin' to anyone, but then you started up your site 'n' I figured you were lookin' for someone else."

A half snort, half laugh escaped my lips. "Can I tell you something?"

His large hand smoothed across my cheek, his fingers tanglin' in a few escapee ringlets. "Fo' sho', anything."

"I started GettinHooked.com for you."

He chuckled low and husky at the back of his throat. It made me smile. "Oh, yeah? For me, shortie?"

"Yup. For you. So I could figure out a way to get hooked up with you."

He kissed my brow again, the caress of his lips so sweet. The heat of it lingered for a sec; the memory will last. "Imani, don'tcha know, all ya had to do is look at me 'n' I was yours. You wanted to get hooked, I've *been* hooked on you since the first time I saw you going to your cousin's."

There's this hella whack place between laughter and tears, and I was crazy mixed in it right then. "Boo, you tellin' me I did all this for nothin'?"

"Nah. For this." And those soft lips of his landed on mine. He slanted, swipin' his tongue across mine, pressin' in a little deeper. But the kiss eased off just as my bones were gettin' set to melt. "There's gonna be a time for that. I'm holdin' ya tonight, remember?"

He chuckled as he tightened his hold on me, then laughed again when I yawned.

"It's been a fucked-up night."

"Yep." He kissed the corner of my eye. "But it's gonna be chill, you'll see. It'll be all gravy, shortie." The way he whispered the words into the air so close to my ear, the flutter of his breath shimmered across my skin and made me feel like I could believe him.

"Folks are gonna be mad 'bout Gettin' Hooked being shut down. They been diggin' the hell out of it."

He didn't say anything, but he didn't have to. I already knew he agreed with me, our wild chase after my cousin to 'Zona had proved it, no matter how it'd turned out. "We'll figure…it out…" His words were coming more spaced out, his breaths lengthening, sleep comin' on as fast for him as it was for me.

Curlin' my fingers into his shirt, I pulled myself just a tad closer, his warmth chasin' the night away, his heat makin' my eyelids hella heavy. And as Maurice's even breathing washed across my cheek, my mind went to mush again, like earlier when I was faded. My thoughts drifted from our journey home, to my friendship with Kayla, to all Gram had done for me, then exhaustion won and sle...

CHAPTER 23

It wasn't fixin' to be an easy mornin'; actually, the entire day was gonna end up whack. I knew this from the first second I opened my eyes and glanced at the clock. It was pushing noon, but the single small window in the dorm room was covered with a blackout drape. No sun had crept in and the room was still dark and cool.

We'd all overslept despite wantin' to be up so we could creep out of 'Zona just as we'd crept in—quick 'n' be done with it. Except on our return trip we had planned on leavin' early enough that we wouldn't have to spend the night out on the road. That plan was probably shot to hell since Maurice was our only driver and the day was half gone already.

And with Kayla along for the return journey, I hella dreaded spendin' a night in a telly again. I clenched my jaw, my body filled with tension, the remainin' resentment I was havin' trouble gettin' over.

How could my girl do me like that? How could Gram?

My shoulders were a little stiff, the need to stretch tuggin' hard at me, but with Maurice's big muscular body takin' up most of the narrow bed, there was no place to move without fallin' smack on the floor.

The weight of his arm had grown heavy on my waist, long fingers seepin' down to curve over my hip. Once I'd fallen asleep it'd been a warm cozy haven in Maurice's arms, but that hadn't been till near dawn. *Not enough time to actually feel rested,* I thought as I stifled a yawn with the back of my hand, then swiped away the escapin' tears from my eyes.

Easin' a foot to the floor, I shimmied from my boo's arms and out of bed, finally able to stretch my achin' shoulders and back. Then a right quick trip to the little girls' room to relieve my poor bladder that was hexa taxed after last night's booze. Something that still had my tummy doin' waves.

Back in the dorm room, I turned on James's computer, then waited for it to warm up. There was somethin' hella strange 'bout sittin' there in the room listenin' to the three of them sleep, knowin' all that I now knew.

There was this big part of me that didn't even feel like the same person I'd been before all this business with GettinHooked.com and my momma, who never really wanted to be my mom anyhow.

Glancin' at the computer screen as Windows loaded, I caught the reflection of my image, wild untamed curls bouncin' every which way around my face, light brown skin, and eyes I knew came from Kayla's side of my gene pool.

I reached for the screen, then pulled away before my fingertips made contact. I'd meant to trace my eyes again, the same way I'd done against the glass the night before, my mind caught up on how similar they were to Kayla's.

And my momma's.

Takin' a deep breath, I shoved away the tears burnin' hella bad at the back of my eyes. I'd said once I wasn't ever gonna cry over her. She didn't deserve it, didn't deserve my sorrow, my pain. She's the one who walked away.

I dismissed last night's sobbin' to having been hexa faded, and those tears had been 'bout betrayal anyhow. Kayla's, Gram's, not my momma's. I was over her. Over missin' her. I wanted to forget 'bout all the lingering questions over why she straight left me.

Turning slightly, I shot a glance at my cousin sleepin' tucked against James on the narrow single bed. Part of me wanted to stomp over to the bed and shake her ass hard, demand to know why she'd spent my entire life lying to me. I tugged in a breath and gripped Maurice's jacket. I tossed the jacket over my bare shoulders, to keep my hands from trembling.

But there was a big part of me that was trippin' hard, wanted like crazy to go back to the way things were. Or at least to be able to figure out how to get over all the whacked shit that had gone down.

Part of me wanted to forgive. Forgive Kayla for not tellin' me that she saw my momma, and how often. Forgive my gram for knowin', too, and providin' my momma with pics of me over the years. Like the woman gave a shit.

And on top of forgivin', I wanted to forget. I wanted so hella bad to forget that my brain was going dumb with it.

I needed time to let it all settle. Needed time to sort shit out.

The computer bleeped to let me know the operating system was ready, yankin' my attention back to it and away from my cousin. Remindin' me that lyin' kinfolk wasn't the only problem I still had to work out.

Openin' up a page right quick, I logged onto Gettin-Hooked, my breath still in my lungs as I watched the profile numbers roll into place. Crap. Holy crap. I squeezed my lids closed, then opened them again.

We'd pushed over five grand now, and as off the chain as that was, it was too outta pockets for two teen girls who'd just been lookin' for a way to find prom dates for themselves and their friends.

I mean, dayum, we were in a dorm room a state away

from home. "Shhhiiiittt," I murmured, droppin' my forehead into my palms.

"Imani? Can we talk?" It was Kayla's soft voice, thick with sleep, and sincere. I knew her well enough to hear the remorse in her tone even without lookin' at her face or big blue eyes.

I shook my head. Hell nah, I wasn't ready for this.

"I'm sorry, Imani." She waited a sec. "I didn't want to hurt you."

But she had. The pain of knowin' she'd known all this time was hexa sharper than the pain of knowin' my momma had been within reach all this time and done nothin' to see me. I inhaled, catchin' the scent of the stale alcohol and Maurice's cologne mingled up on my skin.

"Not right now, K." I swallowed, 'cause the lump in my throat was makin' it hard to talk. "I really don't wanna do this now, aiight."

"Okay," she whispered, and I could hear the way her emotions caught on the single word.

Usin' my fingertips, I swiped away any remainin' moisture from my eyes before I lifted my head. I didn't want her knowin' I'd been cryin'. Again.

"Is there a way we can close down the site from here?" I angled the computer toward her.

She shook her head, sending long blond strands flying. "I don't think so." She slid from the bed and knelt beside me. "Lemme see. We might be able to at least freeze it up so no one else can add until we get home and get access to my dad's server."

"Freeze it up, then."

She nodded, her fingers flying across the keys as she logged in. After a sec, she paused and looked at me. "Hey, Imani, do you think maybe there's a way we don't have to shut it down completely?"

I sucked air between my teeth. I didn't wanna fight with her, but I was already on the edge of losin' my temper hella bad. She must have sensed it, too, 'cause she rushed to go on.

"I'm just sayin', it was a good idea. The whole local-only prom date thang. What if there was some way we could make it be just that? Could we keep it then, ya think?"

"I don't know, K."

"Like if my dad could help us with some security program or sumpthin'?"

I shrugged. "Lemme think 'bout it."

She nodded, her clear blue eyes fixed on mine for a minute. I could see myself mirrored in the shimmer of her pupils. Could see all this emotion, and it was hella weird, because we were able to read each other so well.

And we just sat there like that for a sec, her kneelin' beside me, us starin' at each other, tryin' to get back to the chillness we'd always had.

It wasn't until I heard Maurice stir on the bed behind me that I broke my gaze from my cousin's and glanced over my shoulder in time to see Maurice feel around on the bed for me with his eyes closed.

Grinnin' like a damn fool, I looked back at Kayla. "You gotta pack or anythang? I'm ready to shower, 'n' roll."

Her shoulders heaved, but she nodded, then turned away from me, headed back toward the bed and James.

I kinda wanted to give them a little bit of time alone, to say goodbye and all, 'cause the truth was, there was a pretty good chance they'd never see each other again and I felt bad for her. My man was goin' home with us, hers was staying here.

We were kinda silent, but filled with understandin' as Maurice and I gathered up our stuff, then headed toward the community bathrooms to get cleaned up and changed. After that, things just sorta flew by.

We'd met back up in the hallway about thirty minutes later, me out of my hoochie clothin' and back in sweats and ready for the road.

We headed for Maurice's car, puttin' our stuff into the trunk, then slid into our seats silently. He smiled at me, his hand findin' mine as he laced our fingers, and lounged back in the seat to wait.

It was oddly intimate to sit in the quiet of midday sunshine on the mostly deserted campus. Though we hadn't gone all the way—yet—we'd shared a lot, become so close over the last few days. I knew nothin' was gonna change that even when we were home.

This was the fella I was supposed to be with.

But the time sittin' there just kinda sealed the deal, just highlighted the fact that he'd been the one there for me, the one to hold my hand and brush away my tears.

"Thank you, boo," I whispered, anglin' on the seat so I could peep out his face.

His eyes were closed and I knew he was as tired as I was and facin' a long drive. But his dimples deepened and his lids slowly lifted, revealin' deep dark eyes. "I'd do anythang for you, shortie."

"You were there for me."

"Always will be."

I swallowed, then moistened my lips. "I…" I'd meant to say more, but Kayla was tappin' on the trunk so she could put her stuff in.

After a slow start, things started jumpin' off. Maurice and I were out of the car sayin' our goodbyes. The fellas exchanged cell numbers, then gave a pound. James hugged me, which was a little weird.

Then Maurice and I were back in our seats and Kayla was left outside with James. I knew they were kissin' probably for the last time, so I didn't try to hurry her up, but let her do her thang.

It didn't take long.

Just after one-thirty, we were on the road for home. Maurice, Kayla and I. He was still so hella fiiiinne. She was still my cousin, and my best friend.

We were the same peeps as we'd been before. Everything was the same. And everything was different, too.

CHAPTER 24

WE were just a few hours south of The Bay—home—now, the towns slippin' by fast and blurry. Just midday, the sun was makin' a whack-ass attempt at peekin' through the daily Pacific fog, but at the least the air was moist, so different than 'Zona, where we'd spent the last couple of days.

The closer we got, the bigger the ball of nerves tightening up in my gut. Things weren't figured out yet, and when I rolled back into the hood there was still a hella lot of junk for me to sort through. Drama that wouldn't quit two-steppin' across my mind.

Mostly my relationships with my fam. It's hard to hear the answers and at the same time know deep down that the decisions they made were made out of love. To want answers, but also want things to go back to the way things were before the truth about my momma was revealed.

Takin' a breath, I pulled down the visor and adjusted the angle of the mirror so I could peep Kayla sittin' in the backseat. Her blond hair was pulled back into twin French braids I'd done for her that mornin', and her wide eyes were turned to watch the scenery as we passed, just as I'd been. Reminding me just how similar we were.

There was an ugly weird thang between us right 'bout now, and though I loved this girl—she was my cuzzo, my blood, my heart—I'd be lying if I said shit wasn't strained. I was deeply hurt, but at the same time, we'd always been so close, and I hella wanted the tightness of our relationship back.

Though, I have to admit, last night helped mend the gap some. We ended up havin' to stop at a hotel again, even though we'd hoped for a straight-through drive. Kayla and I were able to sleep in the car while Maurice drove, but he'd had as little sleep the night before as I had. He was hexa drowsy behind the wheel.

So we'd checked into a telly room, puttin' the cost on my card again, knowing there was plenty of cabbage to cover it, though explainin' to my daddy later wasn't gonna be easy. I could only hope he didn't look too close at what I was spendin' his grip on.

The room was a double, two queen beds. Kayla was gonna take one, while Maurice and I cuddled up in the other, but it was only a quick little sec before my boo drifted off to deep sleep and my cousin and I were left with nothin' but the local Bakersfield news, which hella wasn't local to us.

So I'd climbed out of bed with Maurice and climbed in with her. We pulled the blankets up over our heads the way we used to do when we were little and had secrets to share.

And damn, I mean dayum, they weren't secrets, but she did have lots to share. Back in 'Zona, I'd looked for this opp, but someone was always around, so this was our first quiet alone time since she'd bailed. And there were so many questions about James and what had happened between them that I was trippin' over and dyin' to ask.

Startin' with the hickies I'd seen tatted across her skin, right down to the loss of her virginity. I already knew that had gone down, I just wanted to make sure my girl was cool with it. And that they'd used protection.

So in the dimness of our comforter-covered world, my anger slipped and we just became who we were, cousins and best friends. That part was so easy, so comfortable for us.

So I asked the questions, and my girl rolled out the answers. "Did it hurt?" was the first thang I wanted to know, followed by "You all right, girlie?"

And tears were spilled. Not for the reasons I first

thought, but she cried because she didn't feel any different. She thought she would. Thought stars of wonder would explode, thought she'd feel altered in her skin. Older, more mature or some shit like that. But she was just the same old Kayla, and what had started as perfect and special for her was plain and over kinda quick.

When she was through spittin' about James, we moved on to rehash what had gone down in the club, and how Maurice had claimed me as his girl, then tussled over it. And while she explained how she saw it go down, I couldn't wipe this silly-ass grin from my face.

We even talked about MySpace some, how we missed parts of it, of not being in charge and lettin' somebody else handle it.

After a while, I noticed that we avoided talkin' about what had happened after. What had been exchanged between us while looking into that reflection, only showing features but not bright enough to highlight the differences of our skin.

And so we dozed like that, cuddled into our bed cave, just as we'd done since we were just itty-bitty girls.

In the mornin' we hit the road again, and since then it'd been a quiet ride of beats and rhymes on the radio, us shifting stations as we shifted through towns toward home.

I was still lookin' in the visor mirror at Kayla when she turned away from the window and caught me starin'. Her blues locked on mine, and *powww*—there it was, the old understand. The instant knowledge of whatever whacked emotion I was feelin'.

"I'm sorry." She formed the words with her lips, but didn't make a sound.

And my vision blurred with tears right quick. I knew she was sorry. I felt it down to my bones. Squeezin' my lids hella tight, I took a couple deep breaths before I looked back at her.

"You think your dad can make some kinda password or somethin'?"

Her eyes went so round I almost laughed. "Prolly. If he can, you think we can keep Gettin' Hooked goin'?"

I bit my bottom lip as I glanced at Maurice. He'd been watching the road, but must have felt my eyes on him, 'cause he turned my way and smiled so cute it made my insides go warm.

I turned my gaze back to the visor so I could see Kayla's reflection, and I nodded.

"I still need a prom date," she whispered.

"I know."

Maurice took my hand. "You don't."

Nah, I didn't. Not anymore. From Gettin-Hooked.com I'd gotten exactly what I wanted. I had my man. My girls still needed the opp to feel what I was feelin', to hook up with a hella fine brah who makes 'em feel as good as being with Maurice made me.

"Thank you, Imani."

"For what, girl?"

Kayla giggled lightly. "For comin' after me. For bein' my girl." She swallowed. "For forgiving me."

A big ole fat lump formed in my throat and I had to swallow a couple times to clear it out. I flashed her a smile, but quickly turned away, leanin' my forehead on the cool window glass, my hand still warm in Maurice's.

I'd forgiven Kayla because her actions had been done with love. So, then did I need to hold on to the bitterness and anger I was feeling toward Gram and Daddy? For my auntie, the sister of my deserting momma?

Who was at fault here? My grandmother had done what she'd felt was right, always resentin' my momma's lack of care, but still always tryin' to provide me with that relationship. And I hella wondered how much did my daddy even know.

If I confronted them, there'd be pain and tears and anger. What would it serve? And shit, the truth was, did any of it matter? They all loved me. My uncle, my auntie, my cousins. My grandmother and grandfather before he died. My daddy fo' sho'.

The only one who'd failed was the one who'd left me.

The one who didn't deserve me. Didn't deserve to get enough credit to come between me and my real family. The family who was part of my life every day.

Lookin' out the window, I could see my wild curls and wide dark eyes. I could even catch a glimpse of my skin tone, the light brown sugar and honey, the silver streaks of tears trailin' on my rounded cheeks.

I sniffed them up, which Maurice must've heard, because his fingers tightened reassuringly just to offer a little comfort.

I never had my momma's love. And ya know what, I don't want it or need it. I had Maurice. I had my family still, all there to support me. And most important, I have me.

I love who I am, and who I'm gonna be.

Keep that, and I had everything.

KIMANI trn™

She's got attitude…

Keysha's Drama

Bestselling author
Earl Sewell

When sixteen-year-old Keysha Kendall is sent to live with the father she never knew, she finds herself in a fancy house in middle-class suburbia. But Keysha can't forget where she came from and she won't let anyone else forget either. So she hooks up with a rough crowd and does whatever she wants… until what she wants changes real fast….

"Earl Sewell has a knack for creating memorable characters and scenes in his novels that stay with the reader long after they've read the last page."
—Rawsistaz Reviewers

Coming the first week of May
wherever books are sold.